MW01717424

The Faustian Pact by Antony Beevor

For Reasons of State by Antony Beevor

The Whistle Blower by John Hale

The Third Truth by Michael Hastings

The Oxford Gambit by Joseph Hone

The Private Sector by Joseph Hone

The Valley of the Fox by Joseph Hone

The Ninth Man by John Lee

But We Didn't Get the Fox by Richard Llewellyn

The End of the Rug by Richard Llewellyn

The Cooler by George Markstein

Exchange of Clowns by Theodore Wilden

Also by Antony Beevor

For Reasons of State

The Faustian Pact

ANTONY BEEVOR

COLLIER BOOKS
Macmillan Publishing Company
New York

This is a work of fiction. Names, characters, places, and incidents are either the product of the author's imagination or are used fictitiously. Any resemblance to events or persons, living or dead, is entirely coincidental.

Copyright © 1983 by Antony Beevor

First published in 1983 in Great Britain by Jonathan Cape Ltd.

All rights reserved. No part of this book may be reproduced or transmitted in any form or by any means, electronic or mechanical, including photocopying, recording, or by any information storage and retrieval system, without permission in writing from the Publisher.

Collier Books
Macmillan Publishing Company
866 Third Avenue, New York, NY 10022

Library of Congress Cataloging-in-Publication Data
Beevor, Antony, 1946–
The Faustian pact/Antony Beevor.—1st Collier Books ed.
p. cm.
ISBN 0-02-030461-7
I. Title.
PR6052.E323F3 1989
823'.914—dc20 89-7329 CIP

First Collier Books Edition 1989

10 9 8 7 6 5 4 3 2 1

Printed in the United States of America

For the inimitable P. L.

About the Author

Antony Beevor was born in 1946 and educated at Winchester, Grenoble, and Sandhurst. After five years in the British army, he worked in a variety of fields and later became a student of Spanish and South American politics. *The Faustian Pact* is his second political thriller. His first, *For Reasons of State*, is also available as a Collier Spymaster.

I

The wind buffeted against the side of the Land Rover. 'Bloody Wales,' the driver remarked, pointing his chin at the storm clouds over its border. 'Rainiest bloody October I can remember.'

Jamie Maclaren, the young officer beside him, acknowledged with a suitable expression. He twisted in his seat to check the other long-wheel-base Land Rovers; the adjutant had issued new instructions for the close-quarter teams' transport. The driver noticed Maclaren's precaution with a grin. 'Seems as if they want to wrap your lot up in cotton wool, don't it?'

'The crackdown wouldn't have been necessary,' Maclaren replied, 'if some of your muckers didn't dash around like frustrated Grand Prix champions. A whole team's training was messed up as a result of that last smash.'

'But just one of 'em broke a walking out finger!'

Maclaren breathed out sharply. 'It was his right one. Next to his trigger finger.' He felt that the drivers took advantage of the informality which should belong to the teams alone. With slight distaste he eyed the trooper's profile. His cheeks were pock-marked with extinct pimples. A face like a grenade range; that was how they described a girl with a rough complexion. The hair was greasy and the beret had been shaped down tanky-style over his ears to simulate the perpetual wearing of earphones. Maclaren had observed the drivers contort themselves in front of their vehicles' wing-mirrors giving their headgear a slight forward tilt. It reminded him of Teddy boys combing up their quiffs in the reflection of a shop window.

On arrival at the Pontrilas camp, the Land Rovers parked in a line on the asphalt. A gust nearly wrenched the door from Maclaren's grasp as he swung out his legs. The wind roared in his ears. He turned, leaning his shoulder against the window to force the catch shut. What a God-forsaken place, he thought at the sight of the sheep-cropped hills beyond the barbed wire. There was Welsh Wales and there was Army Wales, where the weather always seemed that much more foul.

The QMSI small-arms instructor stood waiting for them by the double doors which resembled the emergency exit of a cinema. 'Right, get yourselves inside,' he ordered as the rest of the troop jumped from the backs of the vehicles. The sixteen men filed into the badly-lit corridor which smelt of damp concrete. There they removed the camouflage combat kit that concealed the black jumpsuits nicknamed 'Milk Tray order' after a chocolate commercial. Once they had hung up their gear they pulled on black balaclavas. Then they collected their Heckler & Koch machine pistols from the REME armourer, who had laid them out on a narrow table.

The QMSI told them to line up in their pairs by the door which led into the Ghost Train. Inside the tall structure, movable walls could be arranged to imitate particular buildings. And the instructors in their box of bullet-proof glass above the maze could open doors by remote control to reveal more dummy terrorists.

'Come on, settle down,' the QMSI called in a tone of wearied patience. He was a boney-faced Lancastrian, erect and unhurried in well-fitted combat kit. 'The colonel's up there to see how you're coming along, so we haven't got all day.' With the armourer he moved down the line, issuing magazines. 'This afternoon we're going to try the ground-floor layout again. And this time I want none of that five-rounds-in-your-own-time business. It's doubled taps into the torso. And then *move*! Right, get ready the first two pairs, and watch for the warning light.'

'Hey, Q!' one of the troopers at the far end called. 'When are you going to get that electronic score-board up in the control room?'

'I wouldn't be so eager about it if I were you, Jeffries. Not after that last performance of yours. Nearly blasted a Very Important Hostage to bits, you did. Any more like that and we'll send you back to playing Space Invaders down the amusement arcade.'

'Come off it, Q,' Jeffries complained. 'I did all right.'

The QMSI flashed him a look of sarcastic sympathy before turning to address the troop. 'By the way, I'm sure you'll all be dead chuffed to hear that we might be getting some new kit.'

'Three guesses, Q?' Jeffries asked, reluctant to lose his attention.

'You'd need three million, lad.' The QMSI glanced up again to check the panel of lights above the door. 'I've heard tell that Madame Tussauds are going to provide us with some heads.'

'Madame Tussauds? You're winding us up again, Q.'

'No shit, as our friend from the Black Berets would say.'

'What?' Jeffries persisted. 'From the Chamber of Horrors?' The QMSI regarded him, shaking his head at such a hopeless case. 'Jeffries, I'm going to have to ask the MO if he can do anything to stop your verbal squitters. You're worse than my ten-year-old. As I was saying, we'll be getting a selection of heads. So when the dummies are switched around, you'll need to be nifty on your recognition. And if any joker puts a round through one of 'em, he'll be on stoppages till pension day. They've got to stay virgin.'

The QMSI's manner changed sharply the moment the red warning light came on over the door. 'Gas masks on!' His word of command was much lower and more articulated than that of a drill sergeant. 'First two pairs stand by! With a magazine of twenty rounds . . . *Load!*'

2

David Rayner's office was on the third floor. If he had been able to open the window of opalescent glass and lean out, a brief section of Theobald's Road would have been visible. The Air Ministry block next door shut out any direct daylight, so that side of the building always needed artificial lighting.

As a career diplomat who transferred to the Friends, and now found himself seconded to the new Department of Security Liaison, Rayner had lost count of the offices he had occupied. The white walls around him remained bare except for a map of Europe, virtually useless for practical purposes, yet still an appropriate symbol for the head of the Allied Liaison Group. With faint amusement, Rayner thought that at least it had a more cosmopolitan look than those of the United Kingdom in his colleagues' offices. He gazed at the group leave roster pinned up beside his desk. The holiday season had now run its course, but in the absence of other charts, he had left it in place.

Rayner still thought about ways to reduce the impersonality of his surroundings, but the options seemed so limited. The set of hunting prints in the spare bedroom at home would appear embarrassingly stereotyped. A framed photograph of his wife would be an obvious possibility. He had always been proud of her looks, but Susie hated his favourite shots which dated from years before when she had tried to model part-time. She seemed to think it an insult to prefer old pictures and insisted that they had never looked like her in the first place.

Rayner felt, however, that on top of security considerations there were good reasons for keeping home and official life apart. The strongest, though least acknowledged, came from an inhibition over personal matters. Most of those who had known him for years never felt it had been with any intimacy.

Few people were surprised to learn that David Rayner had been in the Foreign Office. Even the fair hair streaked with grey and the figure kept trim by squash somehow seemed typical of the middle-ranking diplomat. On the other hand his ready smile lacked the impervious quality of that profession. A cynic might have thought Rayner a man who charmed women easily and exasperated them later. The idea of facile seduction, however, had never really appealed to him.

There was a careless morse tattoo on the door. Rayner immediately recognized the style of his assistant.

'Yes, Nigel?' He raised his eyebrows in an expression of tolerant inquiry as a stocky young man with wavy hair put his head into the room to see if he was free. Rayner found Nigel Pannet somewhat trying.

With his tendency to categorize people, Rayner had always seen Pannet as a rather bumptious little man: almost a contemporary version of the sports car driver who used to sound off in pretentious pubs during the 1960s. Rayner thought that perhaps the whole style was enjoying some sort of revival. Nostalgia fashions seemed to come closer to home every year.

'The Subversive Control Watch Lists, chief.'

'What about them?' He was riled by Pannet's contrived casualness.

'We had them all in except for the West German. They're two days late, which is a touch unusual. I mean, it's been known for the Italians or the Frogs to slip, but not Mr Efficiency in Cologne.'

Rayner stared at him for a moment. 'So what do you want to do? Chase them up by signal?'

'Group status reports are *supposed* to reach the sixth floor by close of play tomorrow.'

Rayner acknowledged the reminder with a sigh followed by a reluctant nod. As he reached across his desk for the black telephone, he noticed Pannet look round for a chair.

Willi Afflerbach, the chief liaison officer in the *Verfassungsschutz*, sounded angry when he answered. Rayner frowned in surprise at such an unusual occurrence; Willi was as polite as he was calm – or stolid, in Pannet's view. Rayner therefore tried even harder to soften the implied criticism behind his inquiry by explaining the requirements of their new status report procedure. He noticed a flash of impatience cross Pannet's face and so switched his gaze to the telephone dial. Rayner's frown deepened in concentration as he tried to catch Willi's abrupt replies.

As soon as the call was over, Pannet wanted to know what the problem was. Rayner paused for a moment before looking up.

'It seems they're suffering from computer gremlins.'

Pannet uttered a cynical laugh. 'Don't we all?'

'Yes. At times. But Willi seemed distinctly perturbed at the scale of theirs.' Finding that his ear tickled, Rayner inserted the tip of his index finger, then agitated it with a brisk swizzling action.

'Knowing the Krauts, I'll bet he was "perturbed",' Pannet said. 'As soon as there's a cock-up in the system, they go into a flat spin. Do you remember the time –'

'Nigel,' Rayner cut him short. 'Just mark the Federal Republic entry as "data not yet provided".'

3

The table had been pushed back to allow more room for the occupants of the two armchairs. The Prime Minister was a large man, and suffered from a back problem which made him stoop slightly. Although hampered by shapeless great suits, he always took pains to present himself tidily, perhaps hoping it would camouflage his ungainly figure and advancing age.

His new political adviser looked even scruffier than the average outsider in Whitehall. But John Simmonds's rumpled appearance was not intended as a statement of non-conformity. He simply felt uneasy in smart clothes, convinced that they made him look ridiculous. Similarly, his hair was long only because he hated wasting time at the barber's. Once or twice he had come out resembling a conscript, all ears, nose and glasses, so as to put off the next ordeal for even longer. Nobody at Oxford cared if he was 'reminiscent of a little cartoon spider with spectacles', as one journalist had recently described him. Simmonds was rueful that such a trivial remark had managed to hurt him, especially since he had always thought politicians over-sensitive to personal comments.

Simmonds glanced at the chrome-framed prints and hessian walls. He felt that the confidentiality of the proceedings, with fastened blinds and subdued lighting, verged on the conspiratorial. But then, he knew that the effectiveness of a presentation depended on its dramatic pitch. In any case, this confirmation of their fears hardly encouraged shouting from the rooftops.

With a prejudiced eye Simmonds observed the market-research consultant indicating the most significant percentages. The man took care not to rap the board. Only a gentle scraping could be heard as the point of the baton moved from one set of figures to another. Between charts, he would place the tip of his middle finger on the bridge of his owl-like glasses, then push them back into position. It reminded Simmonds of a conjuror's automatic flourish at the end of each trick. He then recognized that the presenter's sleekness lay not so much in his business-lunch plumpness, or improbably smooth shave, as in his treatment of the Prime Minister's approval ratings. He managed to make it sound as if they were examining a statistical abstraction, not a wave of dissatisfaction with the person he was addressing.

Simmonds cautiously examined the Prime Minister's profile to check the reaction, but saw only the same expression of cold indifference with which he faced an attack in the House. Private Office called it his old Stonewall look. There was little of that homely crinkling round the eyes which appeared on the posters. And yet Simmonds knew him to be far from passionless. The Prime Minister cared deeply for the Party. He regarded himself as one of its great stalwarts and the guardian of its ideals. Despite his middle-class origins and Oxford education, he tended to come across as a blinkered old unionist, decent and plodding, with unshakeable gut feelings.

The presenter lifted the last chart of the section over the top of the board. 'Now, the question of a possible general election, which we were commissioned to examine.' This acted as a signal for his audience to rearrange themselves in their chairs.

The new sheet announced 'Priority of Issues and Policy Appeal' in large red letters. Jesus, Simmonds thought dejectedly. It really is just like an advertising launch. The door-to-door sampling had already made the Party Leader sound like a celebrity whose image was no longer good enough to continue endorsing the brand.

The press had made much of divisions within the Cabinet and the Party. There were fresh rumours of a breakaway led by the Prime Minister's *bête noire*, whom he was known to hate even more than the Leader of the Opposition. But Simmonds felt that such a suggestion was seriously mistaken. The Prime Minister's opponents knew that he could not hang on much longer, and there was no obvious successor amongst his supporters. The Home Secretary, the PM's most loyal lieutenant, enjoyed neither a strong position within the Party nor popular appeal.

Now that some of the non-aligned members of the Cabinet felt that the leadership question should be resolved quickly, exaggerated reports of the Prime Minister's poor health were circulated by his opponents. Simmonds noticed signs of a growing persecution complex as a result. And only a close circle of confidants had been informed that their chief was considering the unthinkable: a snap election during a period of industrial unrest and demonstrations against unemployment. Simmonds had privately dubbed it the kamikaze option.

While some of the presenter's jargon entered his subconscious, Simmonds wondered how close the whole electoral process had come to a ritual contest between two personalities programmed up to the eyeballs with the right platitudes. It seemed a bad joke that he of all people should be sitting there, particularly since his appointment as speech-writer had stemmed from a jibe against the Opposition's image-makers. But he was forced to admit that losing one's self-honesty – the first casualty of ambition – was always easier to accept with a good dose of ideological morphine.

Simmonds's quips had first attracted the Prime Minister's interest at a dinner in his old college after receiving an honorary degree. Luckily none of the young don's colleagues had been tempted to repeat his aphorism that MPs were eunuchs in the harem of state power. The Prime Minister had talked to him again over coffee, then he had found himself accompanying the great man to the gents'. As they stood at the urinal discussing Ramsay MacDonald, Simmonds found it necessary to suppress a slightly drunken giggle. Remembering that Lyndon Johnson used to pronounce on foreign policy from the john, he decided that the phrase 'corridors of power' should be amended.

After the presentation was over, the marketing consultant opened the door for them. The Prime Minister's bodyguard waited just outside with his right hand holding his left elbow. Simmonds wondered whether they were taught special positions for informal moments. He always tried to make private fun of the security machine because it made him feel so ill at ease. On his appointment, he had suggested facetiously to his wife Nancy that the vetting procedure probably wanted to check on how many times a week he had masturbated at school.

'Do you need dropping off anywhere, John?' he was asked.

'No, I'm fine thanks, Prime Minister.' The title continued to sound strange.

'Well, if you can have a think about that lot. We'd better talk about it as soon as possible.'

'Yes, of course, Prime Minister.'

'Right then. Good night.'

The bodyguard stirred to follow. Simmonds avoided his incurious stare with embarrassed cowardice. He never knew if he was expected to talk to them.

Depressed and longing for a bath, John Simmonds opened the front door of their house in Islington. Nancy was curled up over a book on her emerald-green sofa. John had never really liked the American taste for bright greens and white. He saw it as a mania for reconstituted nature, like Astroturf or painting *trompe l'oeil* skies in bathrooms.

'Hi!' Nancy called, stretching elaborately. She bent forward to lay her book face down on the table. 'I've just sent the kids to bed.' She pushed herself up to greet him. Even without shoes she was taller. Simmonds despised himself for having been once so embarrassed by their difference in height. He had ruled out a church wedding on the grounds of his 'convinced agnosticism': the prospect of everyone watching them come down the aisle had conjured up all those jokes about battleaxe brides carrying spindly husbands over the threshold. Yet apart from a solid jaw, Nancy bore little resemblance to such caricatures.

Her open expression and wholesome looks, which seemed almost to radiate good health around her, had led to him calling her Goody Two Shoes on occasion. She took such teasing easily, aware of the envy it concealed. His favourite image from Massachusetts days was a lightly suntanned Nancy playing a tennis shot with the short laugh he labelled her karate cry.

Nancy was tougher than her appearance suggested. But he had hurt her seriously once by pointing out that her liberal WASP earnestness showed itself most in conversation with blacks. His jibes about sincerely insincere Americans and the Great Mutual Admiration Society were fresh in her memory at the time. Afterwards he developed a guilty suspicion that this incident had made Nancy defensive about politics.

Once John had tucked up the twins and taken a quick bath, he joined her in the kitchen. 'You don't think they're watching too much TV, do you?'

'What do you mean?' she replied without turning round.

'Oh, it was just that Tommy kept chanting some commercial jingle.'

'They're Electronic Age kids,' she shrugged, handing him a bottle of wine to open.

With slow movements he twisted the corkscrew in before clamping the bottle between his knees. He was thinking how such a remark from Nancy would have been unimaginable when they first met in Nixon days. There had been something attractively unreal about the gawky radical from a rich eastern background. But then he had found that life on campus lacked any connection with everyday existence. It was the start of a suspicion that universities were little more than Disneylands of the intellect.

Like many students, Nancy had disapproved of the visiting lecturer's irreverence while secretly envying it. Oxford seemed to be one of the few British institutions for which anyone over there retained any respect. Even his barbs against the executive professors with their Samsonite briefcases had been tolerated as a traditional eccentricity.

'What's got into you?' she asked eventually, after they had eaten in silence for several minutes. He looked up with a laugh and stopped playing with his wine glass. 'Oh, the presentation this evening I suppose.' Nancy smiled to herself at this coy preliminary and waited for him to unburden fully.

After he had described it all, she shook her head. 'You know, underneath all the flip cracks, you're just a corny old romantic. Sure it's a bit sick, but then if the other side does it, you've got to do it too.'

'Never heard you say such a thing in the old days.'

'That was a bit different.'

He was about to disagree,but thought better of it. She looked at him expectantly. 'I don't know,' he sighed. 'I suppose it's because it seemed just another industry. But then everything's industrialized now . . . leisure, sex, religion, politics . . .'

'Is nothing sacred?' she mocked him gently. His only response was a twitch of the mouth. The development of her scepticism had given him mixed feelings.

'Come on, my love,' she said. 'What's happened to that devastating flippancy?' Her husband's need for reassurance and affection never ceased to amaze and amuse her.

'Like that other line of national defence, the English Channel, it's not sure whether it's become obsolete.'

'Oh, they've both probably got a few years yet. Anyway, did you tell the PM what you thought about this presentation?'

'Not yet.'

'I'd just love to be a fly on the wall when you do.'

'You wouldn't stand a chance,' he said gloomily. 'There'd be a bodyguard with an aerosol insecticide at the ready.'

'Seriously, though,' Nancy said. 'Does all this mean you feel I pushed you into it?' Avoiding her eyes, he again started to twist his glass back and forth with the air of a truculent child who was not quite yet ready to relax.

'Yes, you did push,' he replied eventually. 'But that doesn't mean I blame you, or that I regret it necessarily. I probably needed a bit of a shock to the system. Blows away the silken cobwebs of academe, if nothing else.' He half-laughed, looking up at her. 'But what riled me was the way you wouldn't accept my doubts.'

'Okay,' she conceded. 'And you didn't have to call me a closet power groupie.'

'Oh dear, did I really?' He pulled down the corners of his mouth in exaggerated clown-like regret.

Nancy eyed him sceptically as she leant over to take his plate. 'Anyway,' she said, 'just think of all the material for your book.'

'You know, I never worked out whether that justification for taking the job was inspired by you . . . or by me, when I had to give in gracefully.'

Nancy watched him raise a glass to see if it was clean. He laughed self-consciously on noticing her amused expression.

4

'Where did you say you were going with the boss today?' Nancy asked.

'He's addressing the CBI conference,' John said brusquely without looking up from his folded newspaper. Behind the spectacles his eyes were puffed from sleep. Nancy watched him reach out slowly for his glass, put it to his lips, then discover that he had already drained it. Blinking, he looked around the untidy breakfast table until he spied the orange-juice jug behind a cereal packet.

'Oh, Christ, they've finished it all again,' he muttered. 'They must have to stick up their hands to be excused at least five times in the first lesson.'

'Less serious than you up on some platform.'

He was forced to relax his disgruntled expression. 'Cross my legs and think of England.' He yawned, then put a fist to his mouth as an after-thought.

'Anyway, if you really want some more, it's in the fridge.'

He looked at his watch to help him decide. 'Ac-tu-ally, I'd better be makin' tracks.' Americanisms in pukka English had become compulsive. After heaving himself to his feet, he pushed back his untidy hair, but suddenly froze in the middle of the gesture.

'What's it this time?' Nancy asked, assuming that another piece of absent-mindedness had caught up with him. Two days before, he had driven out of a garage with the petrol cap still on the roof of the car.

His hand dropped to his side, 'Nothing . . . Well, it was just that I had that dream *again* about finding myself bald.'

Nancy shook her head in amusement. 'I must remember to ask the next shrink I meet what that really signifies. It's the most inappropriate one I've ever heard.'

'You never can tell. One morning you might just find yourself waking up next to Yul Brynner.'

His joking manner ceased abruptly. He had remembered how part of the dream included a luminous face under a streetlight. 'I'm late,' he said quickly without realizing that his tone implied it was her fault.

Nancy looked back at him perplexed. 'I'm not stopping you.'

He arrived at the Prime Minister's house in Pimlico just before ten o'clock. The PM's wife agreed to stay at Downing Street only when government entertaining demanded. John Simmonds had every sympathy for her attitude. He found the atmosphere of the official residence depressing. Redecoration could not prevent it feeling like a museum.

'The boss must have got out of bed on the wrong side this morning,' the private secretary warned him just inside the front door.

'Am I late?' he asked checking his watch automatically.

'Well, he's asked where you were twice in the last half-hour. There are a couple of points in his speech which he wants to discuss again.' Simmonds made a face at this news, and crossed to knock on the door of the study.

The Prime Minister's new orthopaedic chair looked incongruous next to the heavy Edwardian desk. His wife had finally persuaded him to do something about his back-aches. There was a strong trace of the previous evening's pipe smoke. Simmonds was reminded of the sweet tobacco smell in public lavatories.

'I'm sorry if I'm late, Prime Minister, but the traffic was bad.'

The large man grunted in acknowledgment, then half-turned to look at him with his baleful stare. 'I'm not happy with parts of this speech, you know.'

'Which parts, Prime Minister?'

'These irrelevant bits, which seem to have got tacked on somehow. I'm addressing industrialists, you know, not the unions.'

'Yes, but won't they be paying just as much attention to what you say?'

'Well, on that basis, I might just as well give the same speech to everybody.' Simmonds did not reply, even though a tempting retort occurred to him.

Half an hour later a knock at the door made them both look round. The private secretary appeared with an apologetic air. 'It's time you were thinking of leaving, Prime Minister, but I'm afraid there's a problem with your bodyguard.'

'Where the hell is he, then?'

'He seems to be unwell. He's in the bathroom.'

'That's all I needed,' he groaned. 'What's the matter with this bloody set-up.' He glared at the aide standing uncertainly in the doorway. 'Well, we can't hang about. Get on the phone, and tell them to send a replacement to catch us up, or join us there.'

'But, Prime Minister, the Cabinet instruction on ministerial security . . .'

'For Christ's sake man, do you think I'm not aware of it? Anyway, I won't have it said that I daren't step outside without an armed bodyguard. The escort car's there, isn't it?'

'Of course, Prime Minister, but . . .'

'We're leaving now. John, have you got everything?'

'Yes, Prime Minister.' Simmonds no longer needed to worry about becoming another target now that the outburst of irritation had passed.

They were already by the front door when the private secretary, sounding relieved, announced that the bodyguard had reappeared. Simmonds and the Prime Minister turned to examine his sickly complexion.

'Are you sure you're well enough, Sergeant Carter?'

'Yes, I think I'm all right now, sir. Must've been the curry last night.'

Simmonds was secretly amused when the Prime Minister had to suppress a grimace of distaste after his brief attempt to look sympathetic.

'How are we for time, John?' he asked quickly so as to justify his impatience. He did not appear to listen to the answer while being helped into his overcoat. The private secretary opened the door for them.

'Morning, Tom,' the Prime Minister called to his driver who was waiting by the near side of the black Rover. Tom reacted with what Simmonds saw as the instinctively servile smile of a man enjoying a few reflected rays of glory. With a little award like the BEM and a fund of trivial anecdotes, he could bore family and friends right through his retirement. He wondered what Tom's reaction would be if he was shown a close-up of his face at such a moment. It also occurred to him how easily a leader with socialist pretensions could acquire a taste for the role of *grand seigneur*.

Once Simmonds and the Prime Minister were settled in the back of the Rover, Sergeant Carter climbed gingerly into the front passenger-seat. As a rule he passed the time on duty discreetly kneading a piece of chewing gum into different shapes with his teeth, but on this occasion his cheeks remained motionless. Behind the stoical expression he determined to keep any lingering nausea under firm control.

Tom, the driver, slipped in behind the wheel to buckle his seat-belt with a single practised movement. He was about to make a cheerful comment on the beautiful crisp morning, but his customary glance in the driving mirror to check the Prime Minister's mood kept him silent. He engaged first gear as soon as Sergeant Carter gave the thumbs-up signal to the police car waiting in front.

'When would you like to discuss that presentation we saw, Prime Minister?' Simmonds asked so as to break the uncomfortable silence. He was regarded with surprise for a moment. 'Oh that. Well, let's say Monday.'

Simmonds was about to mention that it would be impossible, due to the parliamentary schedule, but thought better of it.

Simmonds gazed blankly over Sergeant Carter's right shoulder. At the end of the small street the flashing indicator of the police car in front began to mesmerize him. Forcing his attention away he looked instead at the railings and dustbins, then at a man reading a paper outside the newsagent's on the corner. Like a look-out for a bank robbery, Simmonds thought idly.

Tom strained over the wheel trying to see round a parked lorry. He allowed the Rover to inch forward ready to follow the escort car. But as soon as it turned into the main road, the lorry which had hindered his vision accelerated suddenly. It then came to an abrupt halt blocking the end of the narrow street. Tom sounded his horn angrily at the dark-blue mass just in front which cut out much of the light.

Sergeant Carter had also noticed the man outside the newsagent's. When this apparent loiterer looked expectantly down the street rather than at the lorry, the bodyguard twisted sharply in his seat with an instinctive suspicion. His mouth opened to shout a warning, but at that moment a car smashed violently into the rear of the Rover. Sergeant Carter's neck was broken by the impact; the other occupants were stunned.

The man outside the newsagent's threw aside his paper as he dashed for the Rover. His colleague jumped from the cab of the lorry. Another charged across the street having emerged from the back of a green Ford Granada facing in the opposite direction. A fourth member of the gang stayed in the driving-seat revving the engine.

The rear doors of the Rover were wrenched open and the two passengers dragged out. The man from the newsagent's knocked Simmonds unconscious, dropping him across the pavement. The man from the lorry dealt similarly with Tom, once he had managed to release the seat-belt. Then, turning, he helped pull a hood over the Prime Minister's head.

Despite his bulk, the assailants half-carried him to the car on the other side of the street. From beyond the lorry there came the siren and engine scream of the police escort car in high reverse. Within forty seconds of having blocked the street, the attackers were accelerating away with their captive.

The operations room at Scotland Yard had just diverted all available cars to three bomb scares when the alert signal was activated from the escort vehicle. Immediately guessing the connection, the chief inspector felt a sick emptiness in his guts. A few seconds later the codeword confirming the attack was received, together with details of the wanted car.

The operations staff seated with headsets at their consoles eyed the chief inspector. For a moment he felt like an actor who suddenly finds himself on stage in an unknown play. The sergeant on the master panel prompted him by passing the plastic folder which contained the Immediate Action Procedures. The chief inspector stopped himself demanding how the escort car had become separated from its charge. He flicked open the folder, imagining a moment of unnatural calm before every telephone in Whitehall began to ring.

'Right,' he said mustering a firm tone. 'First of all pass the vehicle details to CITRAC and A8.' There was a slight chance that Central Integrated Traffic Control or the public-order unit might pick it out on one of their street monitoring cameras. 'Next, activate the roadblock operation. All stations call. I'll get the staff officer at HQ London District.'

He had a wild vision of the Household Cavalry stopping tourist buses at sabre point. Most police officers had been unhappy about the Army's involvement in a cordon operation. They suspected that the higher echelons at the Yard had been tempted by the idea of commanding a joint operation.

'Who's next?' the sergeant asked.

'Anti-Terrorist Squad,' the chief inspector snapped back. He was furious at having had to explain to the officer at Horse Guards what the codeword meant.

More and more lights flashed on the consoles. The chief inspector renewed his effort of concentration. Afraid that his mind would block, he had broken out in a nervous sweat. Suddenly remembering that the Commissioner was due to leave for a seminar at Bramshill, he tapped out the number of the priority line. Next on the list was the Department of Security Liaison. He gestured to the sergeant to take care of it.

On being informed by his own operations room the director-general had a moment of panic. The new procedures were now in force, and he lacked confidence in the state of readiness of his recently-created organization. His first need was for an expert in anti-terrorist co-ordination.

'Get Sykes to my office immediately,' he told the duty officer, who waited on the telephone for instructions. On replacing the receiver, the director-general remembered that he should have said Commander Sykes, but this was no time to worry about hierarchical finesse. Besides, he was well known for disliking pomposity.

The director-general took pains to distance himself from the image of the secret world's traditional mandarins. He often emphasized that he was not a member of either the Traveller's or Brooks's. Sitting at the end of the boldly redecorated office on the sixth floor, his slightly foreign looks made him seem more like the owner of a successful modern gallery.

The director-general did not particularly like the expressionless policeman who headed SESLIG, the Security Services Liaison Group. But he had to admit that Sykes's rapid arrival was reassuring.

'Take a chair, Dennis,' he said, closing the desk drawer which contained his staff list with first names. 'I presume you've heard.'

'Yes, sir. The ops room warned me.' Sykes adjusted his spectacles and then fixed his attention on the director-general's face.

'Well, as you know, under the new procedures we've got to set up a full meeting of the crisis management committee. Now the Home Secretary . . .' He broke off with irritation to answer the telephone. 'What?' he demanded. 'His *shoes*? You're sure? I see. Thank you.' He turned back to Sykes with a surprised expression. 'Apparently they've found the PM's shoes at the end of the street. The terrorists must have chucked them out of the car window. Now why the hell would they want to do that?'

'I'd've thought, sir, that it was a precaution in case transmitters were concealed in the heels.' The director-general checked his disbelief on noticing the patient expression on Sykes's face. 'It's not new,' Sykes said. Whenever he found it necessary to explain the obvious, his voice flattened as if on automatic pilot. 'In my previous post I made several recommendations that high-risk targets should carry such devices. But not in such obvious places as heels.'

His manner made it plain that those who had ignored the warnings should now be feeling very uncomfortable. The director-general could understand such an attitude in the circumstances, but it did little to help him like the man.

Within three minutes of the Prime Minister's abduction, the SAS team on permanent stand-by in London had been alerted. The operations room at Scotland Yard then rang 22 SAS Regiment at Hereford.

'Colonel!' the adjutant yelled on seeing the commanding officer pass his door.

'What on earth is it, Alistair?' the colonel asked in a pained and weary tone on retracing his steps.

'FLASH GORDON.'

'Jesus Christ! What's happened?'

'Seems the PM's been snatched.'

'FLASH GORDON's Hidden Hostage, isn't it?'

'Yes, colonel.' The adjutant followed the same line of thought. Under the new procedure they were to maintain permanent contact with the Department of Security Liaison. But the moment the discovery of the terrorists' location was announced with the codewords FLASH HARRY, then the crisis committee known by the acronym COBRA would take over in the Cabinet Office briefing room.

'Right, sound the gong and get on that telephone.'

The adjutant swivelled his chair, opened the door of the small box on the wall, and pressed a button. Red lights accompanied by a buzzer were activated in offices all over the camp, as well as at the Pontrilas training base ten miles away.

'You'd also better tell the Kremlin to contact the Department in London. I want a sitrep in fifteen minutes.' The adjutant reached for the telephone to ring the intelligence officer. 'And where's Jamie Maclaren?' the colonel demanded. The adjutant cradled the receiver between head and shoulder while he flipped open his plastic folder to consult the training programme. 'Interrogation refresher in the romper room.'

'Tell him to issue a warning order to his boys. The forward control unit is to leave immediately. The Pagoda team can brief them on arrival.'

Maclaren was one of the last to arrive in the briefing room next to regimental headquarters. The men of his special troop occupied the two front rows. Their squadron sergeant-major, whose sand-coloured beret seemed too small for his large head, was standing by the platform. He gave the young officer a wry grin. Maclaren replied with an expression of mock suffering. Probably everyone in the regiment was jealous of this chance of glory within their own little world.

The CO strode into the room followed by the regimental intelligence officer. There was no calling to attention, but everyone rose to his feet. The colonel was the only officer accorded formality. Once on the platform, he wasted no time.

'Knowing how fast word gets round, there's probably no need for me to tell you that the Prime Minister's been snatched in London by terrs. As yet we have damn all to go on. They got clean away despite roadblocks all over the place. In fact it looks as if that rather vital part of the contingency plan was an utter balls-up. So all we can do for the moment is prepare.' The colonel turned to the officer detailed to lead the Advance Liaison Group. 'Same as last time. Straight to Chelsea, where you will remain on standby and in permanent contact with the police ops room. It may be a bit of a wait, but I hope to God for everyone's sake that they come up with something pretty soon.'

'Next, the main assault group.' The CO looked along the front row, instinctively checking the expressions of Maclaren's men. 'The last thing I want is you lot sitting in London on your arses getting stale. Instead, I'm going to have RAF choppers sent over here to wait till the terrs are located and FLASH HARRY is signalled. So it's back to Pontrilas to keep the eye in, but otherwise everything ready to go at any moment.'

5

On weekday mornings David Rayner rarely saw his wife before he left to catch the 7.47 from Reigate. Susie, one of the most fitful of sleepers, could emerge from her bedroom at any time up to mid-day. The effects of insomnia gave her an air of tough detachment first thing in the morning. Once, on catching sight of herself in the mirror at the foot of the stairs, she had said in a mixture of self-mockery and wishfulness: 'There's that lean resilient blonde who's really *lived*.'

'Of course it must be serious, darling,' she replied to his perfunctory apology for having woken her. 'Particularly if you're prepared to risk being late in at the Department.' She turned her face towards the kitchen window and blinked at the brilliant sky. 'But since "meaningful communication" is difficult at this sort of time, wouldn't it be better to leave it till the evening?'

'You're hardly in the mood when I get home.'

Susie gave an amused grunt. 'Is that a cowardly way of saying I'm usually pissed?'

'No. I was only quoting your standard excuse whenever I do want to talk about anything important.'

With an elbow on the formica table, Susie propped her chin in her hand to stare back at him. 'I will give you one thing, David.'

'What's that?' he said, masking suspicion with tolerant resignation.

'I've never actually heard you describe something as "not unimportant". And that must be some sort of record.'

'Sorry to disillusion you, but we don't spend the whole day dreaming up new double negatives. Anyway, shall we go and sit in the drawing-room?'

'Do we have to be so ridiculously formal? It's freezing in there. And besides, I need some more coffee. Anyone would think you were about to announce some deeply momentous news . . . You're not going to have a baby are you?'

'Oh, for Christ's sake!' The tone of weary disappointment had become unconvincing with repetition. He was certain Susie felt he tried to thwart her enjoyment of life. And to prove her point, she often set out to force him into disapproving stances. It was all supposed to show how he was no longer the 'fun person' she had known.

Rayner was convinced that his great mistake dated from before their marriage when he failed to knock any romantic visions of diplomatic life firmly on the head. Perhaps like other embassy wives, she had daydreamed secretly of charming ambassadors and vital discussions at their dinner table. The subsequent disillusionment could hardly have been helped by the chief hens treating the subject brightly, as if it was one of those silly but unavoidable problems of growing up, like 'pashes' at boarding school. Susie had reacted in a perhaps predictable way, with an indiscreet affair, heavy drinking and intentionally provocative behaviour at receptions. The Foreign Office had only been prepared to offer him a desk job in London on the clear proviso that his wife never attended government functions again.

'Well, I'm listening.' Susie tapped her cigarette ash into the saucer of her coffee cup, then looked up at him in a pointedly expectant way. Although an old trick of hers, it could still put him off balance.

Rayner gave a resolute sigh. 'Look, I've had another letter from the bank.'

Susie uttered a weary laugh. 'Don't tell me the whole dramatic build-up was just for another little lecture on extravagance. It's not surprising we're so overdrawn. That massive exercise in false economy of moving out here to glorious Repro-Land might have some bearing on the subject. Because apart from being right out in the

Boonies, Woodside Close was hardly a "clever" buy from any point of view . . .'

'I'm not going over that again. The point in question is our current expenditure.'

'Like our taste in cars? Perhaps you're going to tell me about your new little toy's fuel economy.'

The telephone began to ring. Rayner muttered a curse as he pushed himself to his feet.

'Well, leave the bloody thing!' she said, bringing a cigarette up to her lips.

'It might be the office. I told them to ring if anything important cropped up.'

'Everything seems to be important this morning. Be careful, darling; that's the sign of the bureaucrat needing to inflate his little ego.'

Determined to ignore her jibe, he strode angrily out to the hall. 'Rayner speaking,' he answered, then realized that Susie would mock the official manner.

'It's panic stations.' Rayner recognized the voice of his assistant. 'The PM's been snatched. Crisis meeting starts in an hour.'

'Oh Jesus,' he breathed aghast, but Pannet had already hung up. Rayner's immediate reaction was horror at having chosen that morning to go in late.

At every corner in the back lanes, Rayner sounded the horn of his Lancia, braked then accelerated. Much of the time he drove leaning forward while he retuned the radio from one station to another. A van coming in the opposite direction took him by surprise. He was forced to swerve as the other driver hooted furiously. The sudden danger made him feel weak for a moment, but his nervous compulsion for speed over-rode everything.

The pop record on Radio One exasperated him. He glanced at his watch between gear-changes, and swore on seeing that the next headlines were not due for another twenty minutes. But just as he reached the Reigate road, the music was stopped for a newsflash. 'We have been informed by Scotland Yard that the Prime Minister's car was attacked by terrorists in central London a short while ago, and that he has been kidnapped. Roads within, and leading out of, the capital have been sealed by roadblocks. Motorists are advised not to attempt any journey in the Greater London area for the next few hours due to the need to search every vehicle. Traffic has been brought to a virtual standstill. We will bring you further details the moment they become available.'

The full import of the new crisis management system did not strike him until police sirens forced over the taxi he had taken from the Underground station. He recognized the Home Secretary and the Cabinet Office Co-ordinator in the back of a ministerial Rover which was sandwiched between escort cars. With renewed desperation, Rayner urged the cabby to go faster.

The ineffectiveness of the roadblock network was shown when the driver suddenly announced that he knew a good back-double, then flicked round through a complex of sidestreets to avoid a queue. 'They've even got the bleeding Army out,' the cab driver informed him over his shoulder. 'Bunch of woodentops from Chelsea barracks were manning one where I was stopped. Anyway, once I've been and dropped you, I'm going to knock off until things get moving again. Just gives you the hump trying to work when it's like this.'

Rayner was taken aback by the cab driver's attitude, but he was too frantic to argue. The taxi had hardly stopped when Rayner thrust the money down over the cabby's shoulder. Not bothering to close the door behind him, he ran to the main entrance trying to extract his pass from an inside pocket. With relief Rayner sighted Pannet waiting to brief him on the way up in the lift.

'Christ, of all the blasted mornings to be late,' Rayner muttered. 'Has there been any communication from the terrorists?'

'A man phoned Downing Street from a call-box on Waterloo station. Probably pre-recorded on cassette.

Said they were the Red Vanguard and claimed responsibility.'

'Are we certain that – '

'It wasn't a hoax. The terrs chucked his shoes out of the window, but none of that's been released. And now they've given a form of authentication signal in their message, by saying the PM would stay barefoot. Still no demands as yet. I've already fired off signals to allied services. Obviously nothing to go on. More of a warning order, really.'

'Well done anyway. I suppose it's all we can do for the moment. Was anyone hurt?'

'None killed, but the bodyguard's in a bad way. The others were just sandbagged. The terrs rammed from behind and broke the poor bugger's neck. The cunning bastards must have known the front passenger-seat headrests had been removed so as to give the babysitters all-round vision. I'd have thought whoever had that bright idea is going to get shat on from a great height.'

Rayner grimaced non-committally. Pannet seemed to be affecting even more of an off-hand manner in the emergency. The lift came to a halt. Rayner took the dossier with a nod of thanks and turned down the corridor towards the conference room.

The crisis management meeting eventually broke up with the sudden departure of the Home Secretary accompanied by the Department of Security Liaison's director-general and the Cabinet Co-ordinator for Security and Intelligence. As the others present collected up their papers to file out in the wake of their flagships, Rayner gestured to the group head of the Security Services Liaison Group, SESLIG, that he wanted a word with him. Sykes assented with one of his imperceptible nods like a bidder at an auction.

Moving round the table to join him, Rayner marvelled at the lack of animation in the police officer's face. The only exception he could remember was a Pavlovian twitch of disgust once, when someone brought out a packet of cigarettes. The pale smoothness of Sykes's skin reminded him of an uncooked sausage, while the shiny metallic frames of his glasses suited the role of anonymous administrator. A research institute, Rayner thought. The slightly pudgy hands had a scrubbed, sterilized look.

Rayner took the next chair, then leant towards Sykes with his forearm on the table. He glanced round quickly before speaking.

'Listen, I heard yesterday from my liaison counterpart in the *Verfassungsschutz* in Cologne that they've got computer problems.'

'And what did he say caused them?' Sykes asked, still tidying his papers.

'He didn't. But reading between the lines, it would seem that West German security is in a bit of a flap. It was most unlike him to sound so disturbed.'

'Hardly surprising,' Sykes commented quietly, then turned to look at his colleague.

'What do you mean?'

'The Federal Police in Wiesbaden say it was deliberate sabotage.'

Rayner was utterly taken aback. He stared at Sykes for several moments. 'But with this morning's attack that can't just be a coincidence.'

Sykes gave a slight shrug as if to say they should certainly bear a possible connection in mind. But unable to ignore Rayner's impatient reaction, he explained that past experience taught him never to become fixated by coincidences. 'Let's wait until we have the phonetic analysis of the phone call. That might help if there is foreign involvement.'

6

The only colours which stood out in the hospital room were the bright patterned curtains and some yellow chrysanthemums in a pot. Rayner found them morbid flowers. He remembered from his time in France how they were put on family graves for All Saints.

'Well, you must have a good memory,' John Simmonds said in apology for not remembering his visitor. He looked slightly ridiculous propped up in bed. The plaster down his nose with another across under his eyes gave him the air of a helmeted Greek in an amateur production. 'I can't remember many from outside my own college.'

Rayner gave a short laugh. 'Oh, I've got total recall . . . usually of useless facts; I can even remember my different locker numbers at school. Anyway, the Cabinet Office passed us all your details, so it was easy to check you were one and the same.'

'But you're obviously not here to discuss Oxford days . . . though of course it's nice to see you again.'

'I'm afraid it must be very boring for you, but . . . I was wondering if we could go over the attack.'

'The plain-clothes boys have done it so thoroughly already that I don't suppose another go will make much difference.'

Rayner's regretful smile was genuine. The noise of the police guard shifting his weight outside the door exacerbated his unease. When he had suggested to Sykes that he might see the PM's adviser, the reaction was frosty. Victims were evidently regarded as police property. 'As I think I said,' Rayner explained, 'my set-up deals with European security liaison.'

'Is there anything to indicate a foreign tie-in, then?'

'Obviously we can't tell until their demands have been received.'

'Well, they weren't singing "The Internationale" in Serbo-Croat to my knowledge.' Simmonds checked himself. 'I'm sorry. But honestly the whole thing lasted just a few seconds. None of them spoke a word. All I saw was a face appear at the window. The door was yanked open. He hauled me out, and then I got bashed over the head.'

'You wouldn't be able to recognize anything about him?'

'I only noticed that he had a dimple in the middle of his chin. I told one of the policemen. Anyway, it's hardly a distinguishing mark of foreigners.'

Rayner tilted his head. 'Oh well. I'm sorry to have troubled you.' He glanced across at the television with the volume turned down.

'Don't worry,' Simmonds said. 'It's bad enough in here alone with silent Siegfried outside the door for company. Anyway, perhaps you can fill me in on what's been happening.'

'Alarm and despondency. And the odd theory. You heard about the bodyguard feeling sick?'

'Oh yes, the curry.'

'A forensic team, or whatever, went straight down to Pimlico to get a sample of his vomit.'

Simmonds began to laugh. It was the first time he had been lifted out of his apathy since the attack. 'So some poor bloody Indian take-away is going to get ripped apart by armed police. And then in six months' time it'll be prosecuted by a public health inspector. Britain, you have nothing to fear!'

Rayner smiled uncomfortably, wondering whether Simmonds was still suffering from shock. He suggested that perhaps he had better leave.

'No, don't. At least not unless you're in a desperate hurry. Can you turn the sound up on the box? It's the news.'

The ticker-tape signature tune faded as a shot of 10

Downing Street appeared. 'No advance in the search for the terrorists,' the voice-over said. The screen then showed the Houses of Parliament. 'The Commons has just passed a comprehensive programme of emergency legislation. The death penalty is restored for murder arising from an act of terrorism. Habeas Corpus is suspended and identity cards are to be introduced immediately. Messages of sympathy have been coming in from all over the world.'

The announcer looked up at the camera. 'Good evening. This afternoon, the Home Secretary . . .'

'"Comprehensive programme",' John Simmonds murmured. 'They're certainly not mucking about.'

The next morning the hospital rang Nancy to tell her that she could take her husband home. The doctors felt that the small risk of delayed shock would be offset by the reassurance of home surroundings. When she arrived at the hospital, the doctor warned her that her husband might suffer from feelings of guilt for having survived the attack.

'Have you any idea how long this depression could go on for?' she asked. The doctor touched her shoulder as two orderlies approached wheeling a patient down the corridor. 'It really shouldn't be long at all, Mrs Simmonds. It's just something liable to happen in these situations. Try and keep him from listening to the news too much.'

'Yes, but it's not going to be easy. He might start to feel I'm trying to keep things from him.' The doctor nodded sympathetically before assuring her once more that there was no physical damage.

After this conversation she was pleasantly surprised to find that John seemed almost himself again. He was examining the purple marks under his eyes in the mirror over the basin.

'I look like one of those Mandrill baboons,' he commented.

'Well, put your glasses back on. They'll hide the bruising a bit.'

He did not appear to have heard her. 'I must remember to put in an application in triplicate so the government'll pay me for the ones that were broken.' His remark made her feel uneasy again, since it was impossible to know if he was joking. It also brought home to her how difficult it would be to stop him dwelling on the attack.

'They're allowing us to leave from the ambulance bay at the back,' she said. 'There are journalists downstairs apparently.' She noticed him about to make some remark, but then he turned away to check that he had everything. 'I must pick up some papers from the office,' he said.

'But for goodness' sake, you're supposed to be going home to rest.'

'They're only for the book,' he replied.

Outside there was a strong wind blowing the leaves along the pavements.

'Winter is a comin' in,' he recited. Nancy smiled back, but then warned herself against slipping into the cheerful nurse routine. She knew it would only prompt him into deeper glooms. She stared through the windscreen, waiting for him to finish fiddling with his seat-belt. There was no need to look at his face to know that his mouth would be set in uncomfortable resignation to being driven.

As they approached the metal barriers at the entrance to Downing Street, she slowed down. 'Looks like quite a little crowd outside.' Acknowledging her observation with a reluctant grunt, John prepared to climb out.

Although Nancy was unhappy at his insistence on visiting the office, she knew the excuse of missing papers would only encourage him to be restless. She had to restrain herself from asking whether he would be all right on his own.

'I'll only be a few minutes,' he promised. His smile required an effort. 'I know exactly where they are.' He crossed the pavement with his lopsided walk. A gust of wind caught his hair. The irritated movement of pushing it back into place was so typical that Nancy relaxed.

From a second-floor window John Simmonds looked down on the silent crowd spilling off the far pavement. It had greatly increased in size since the terrorists' demands, including the release of political prisoners in Northern Ireland, were made known on the ten-thirty news. Some held transistor radios to their ears listening for the latest bulletins.

On the edge of the crowd he caught sight of two men. One held a bunch of flowers, the other a camera. They were both searching the faces in front of them. Suddenly the man with the flowers gestured urgently to his companion pointing out a woman who held a little girl by the hand. He began to speak to her earnestly. Then he bent to give the girl the flowers while the photographer adjusted his lens. John Simmonds visualized the front page constructed around the shot. Packaged emotions to sell packaged news, he thought angrily.

His coldness towards the crowd below made him fear his lack of feelings, both for them and for the Prime Minister. In his hospital room he had tried several times to imagine what the man was going through at the hands of the terrorists. But the picture was as unconvincing as his memory of the attack.

He attempted to tell himself that the frustration came from being denied his usual escape of flippancy, yet he knew it went deeper than that. He experienced an overwhelming urge to shock the colleagues and staff who had stared at him as if he were a ghost. Recovering their manners, any enthusiasm for his recovery had of course to be subordinated to the gravity of the situation. Geoff, the porter, was the only one to react naturally with a good-humoured remark about the bruises.

Cursing Whitehall in general, John had an even greater desire to be home. Remembering with sudden guilt that Nancy still waited for him in the car, he forgot all about the papers.

7

Once again David Rayner found himself observing the modernizations carried out in the long conference room. It was a typical DoE cosmetic job, he thought. The white walls, the blinds and the charcoal-grey swivel chairs on chrome bases were all in good execucrat taste. The double-glazed windows had been installed as a protection against directional microphones.

Rayner's concentration had started to wander when the Commissioner opened the crisis meeting with tortuous euphemisms for their lack of success. The Home Secretary had shifted ostentatiously in his chair at one point. Rayner suddenly remembered the surprising joke made by a former commissioner that if ever terrorists seized a politician, they should be offered as many others as they could manage. It was hardly something the present incumbent would like to hear repeated.

The man excited little sympathy as he laboured through an obviously prepared statement. Rayner glanced at Sykes who was staring at the blotter in front of him. Heads down when the shit's about to fly, Rayner thought. But Sykes's position was probably very strong after his unheeded warnings. So perhaps he was just being cautious. Never look at your superior when he's making a hash of it; faces remembered after such painful scenes become suspect. Of course the Commissioner should have put someone else in to bat on such an unfavourable wicket. The choice depended on the level of scapegoat required.

With sidelong glances down the table, Rayner observed the Home Secretary lose patience rapidly. According to the press, this irritability combined with his 'lack of charisma' ruled him out as a contender in any possible struggle for the Party leadership. With functional glasses, a lined face and spiky black hair, he resembled a 1950s schoolmaster who cared little for popularity. Someone in Five had commented that he was humourless enough to make a first-rate commissar. And yet others, often the least expected candidates, came out admitting respect for the man.

'Perhaps, Sir Neil,' the Home Secretary interrupted, 'it might be better if you asked one of your officers to develop in more detail the general picture you've been giving us.'

The Commissioner of the Metropolitan Police could not conceal his surprise, but he immediately designated Commander Don Bailey of the Anti-Terrorist Squad.

Rayner wondered whether the head of 'The Wild Bunch' had learned his lesson from the first crisis meeting, when he had criticized the security precautions surrounding the Prime Minister. Afterwards Bailey must have received a warning from on high that officers who broke ranks in front of outsiders would suffer more than a rap over the knuckles.

Sykes's dead-pan manner might be intimidating, Rayner reflected, but his erstwhile colleague looked distinctly alarming. Bailey possessed what seemed to be the perfect example of a hatchet face. In fact his profile resembled a crude caricature of a gypsy. Rayner could not help thinking that an actor who specialized in criminal roles would seldom be out of work with such features. Sykes and Bailey seemed to be poles apart in more than just manner and appearance. One brief exchange at the last meeting had suggested a deep animosity as well. The police must have their Byzantine intrigues like the rest of us, Rayner thought.

'As the Commissioner made clear,' Bailey said, his eyes flickering over the faces on the opposite side of the table, 'there has been little progress to date.' His restraint, in contrast to the previous occasion, seemed to confirm that he had received a serious warning. To begin with, it appeared as if Bailey intended to bore his audience into apathy. In the greatest detail he covered the examination of the vehicles, the fingerprints found on them, and the analysis of fibre and soil particles as well as samples of human and dog hair. Then he started to cover the different routes which, according to police tests carried out with a similar vehicle, the kidnappers might have taken.

The Home Secretary soon lost patience once more. 'Yes,' he broke in, 'but what can you deduce from all this?'

'Only that they must have known their back-doubles bloody well, sir.' Bailey's reply took everyone aback. Several glanced to check the Home Secretary's reaction, but the Anti-Terrorist chief did not give him time to think up a response.

Rayner examined Bailey with even greater interest, awed by his nerve as he proceeded to list all the other measures taken: the raids on known extremists, the searches, the seizure of address books to help update friendship networks on the computer, the interrogations, and the monitoring of thousands of telephone lines through the System X exchanges. But in all these cases, he emphasized, especially the tapping, where they needed key trigger-words or matched voice-prints to activate the circuit, background information on the terrorist group was still in short supply.

While witnessing Bailey's performance, Rayner wondered whether the Commissioner would be grateful or jealous. Bailey had suddenly shown he did not merit that damning civil service label 'unsubtle' after all. He had succeeded in deflecting the flak away from the police. A glimpse of the director-general's face told Rayner that he was not alone in noticing the dangerous shift in the wind's direction. Of his fellow group heads in the Department, only Sykes seemed unmoved, but then his group did not have a data-gathering function.

Bailey's summary was just as effective. There was little sign of self-justification, even when he spoke of the mass of calls from the public which had to be sifted. 'We can count on some 15 to 20 per cent being either crank or mischievous. Only a fraction of 1 per cent is likely to be of any potential use. The vast majority are well-meaning but erroneous, so there is always the danger of missing the one vital tip-off in the flood.' He paused. 'We are all well aware of what happened under similar circumstances in Germany some years back.' Bailey's eyes no longer moved restlessly. He pretended to rearrange his papers.

'Thank you, Commander Bailey,' said the Home Secretary. His pensive tone made the Department members ill at ease. 'I think we all appreciate the efforts you and your men are making under very difficult conditions.' Bailey was far too much of a professional to show pleasure at such a turn-around.

The Home Secretary stared for a moment at the pad in front of him, even though it was marked with only two small doodles. 'Gentlemen,' he said, raising his head to look around him. His eyes avoided the director-general. 'I, for one, now find the reasons for our grave situation a good deal easier to understand.'

The director-general broke the deliberate silence in a pre-emptive move. 'If I may say so, Secretary of State, I think we are all very conscious that our basic weakness is the lack of data on the terrorist group. But then neither Five *nor* Special Branch has managed to produce raw material for us to analyse.'

The prompt lob back into the other court made Rayner smile to himself in relief, although he was embarrassed at how little he had to pass on to allied services in Europe. The Home Secretary made no attempt to conceal his exasperation. He peered forward angrily at the agenda. 'Well then, let's at least hear your analysis of the terrorists' phone messages. As that now seems to be all we've got to go on.'

Turning to his left, the director-general discreetly ignored the second remark. 'Commander Sykes, would *you* please present the Departmental analysis?' The head of the Intelligence Liaison Group, whose staff had completed the work only twenty minutes before the meeting began, stared in surprise. But since security co-operation was the sole reason for the Department's existence, Sykes with his police background was the obvious choice.

Sykes glanced through INTELLIG's memorandum before shifting forward in his chair. 'The first point, Secretary of State, is that we believe the telephone message received at zero nine forty-three this morning was genuine. The acoustic experts have also confirmed that, like the first message, it was pre-recorded on cassette.' Sykes paused for a reaction from the Home Secretary, and received a brusque nod.

'In our present situation, lacking hard intelligence, their communiqués are even more important as guides. Red Vanguard obviously wants them to be published, so we can probably assume that they reflect their political stance and origins.' Rayner heard the INTELLIG group head on his right give a sigh at the circumspect formulation. The day before, someone in the Department had commented that Sykes would soon have a seat-belt installed on his office chair. But Rayner thought such criticism a little exaggerated. Sykes simply took great pains to avoid any challenge on detail which might distract from the essence of his argument.

Sykes took several minutes before he even began to cover the findings of the linguistic and phonetic analysis. 'The report does make one observation,' Sykes said, his tone emphasizing a need for caution. 'It may either be important, or dangerously misleading.' The Home Secretary stopped staring at his note pad, and raised his head in expectation. 'The report points out the curious formulation of two sentences in particular, which suggests a literal translation from a foreign language.'

'Which language?'

'The construction suggests a Germanic or Scandinavian influence, sir.'

'And what is the Departmental view? Can anything be done to follow up this theory?'

Just as David Rayner was bracing himself to reply, the director-general leant forward. 'ALLIG has kept our West German colleagues informed of all developments including this one, Secretary of State. However, as you can imagine, there is little concrete help they can give us at this stage.'

That's putting it mildly, Rayner thought. With the *Verfassungsschutz* keeping hatches battened down, no mention had been made of the computer sabotage. The last thing they wanted was the Home Secretary on the hot line to Bonn. The Federal Government would go beserk at having been kept in blissful ignorance by its own security services.

'It was clear from the beginning', Sykes went on, 'that the abduction of the Prime Minister was the first part of a two-step operation. It was not obvious, though, whether he was both a primary and an instrumental target at the same time.'

'By instrumental,' the Home Secretary put in, 'I presume you are talking of a lever to force the release of the Irish prisoners. But what do you mean by "primary" in this context? That they want to kill him whether or not we agree to their demands?'

'Not exactly, sir, though it is of course a possibility. We are thinking more of what happened in Italy. That is to say, the interrogation of an important captive to obtain information which might prove damaging to the state.'

The Home Secretary regarded Sykes for several moments. 'I see,' he said, then leant forward to write on his note pad. The director-general waited until he had finished. 'We have already asked the Intelligence Corps interrogation psychiatrists at Ashford to prepare you a report.' The Home Secretary ackowledged this with another curt nod, which also served as a signal for Sykes to continue.

8

'Is it all right if someone comes to supper tonight?' John Simmonds called on hearing his wife come downstairs. He was half-lying along the green sofa he enjoyed being rude about. Nancy appeared in the doorway. She looked surprised for a moment although she had heard him on the telephone.

'Yeah, sure. Who is it?'

'A character called David Rayner. He was a contemporary of mine at Oxford, though I hardly remember him.'

'Well, what's he doing now?' She sat on the arm of the sofa by his feet.

'He was in the Foreign Office, then did the switch to the "Friends" . . . sorry, Secret Intelligence Service,' he added in answer to her raised eyebrow.

'Aren't we joining the Whitehall cryptocracy a little too easily?'

'Hardly.' He made an evasive movement. 'Anyway, he's now head of allied liaison at the Department of Security Liaison. He came to visit me in hospital.'

'How very thoughtful of him.'

John was embarrassed by her irony. 'Well, in fact he wanted to know if there was any chance of the attackers being foreign.'

'They must be pushed if ex-diplomats have to play Sherlock Holmes as well.'

'Frankly, I don't think they trust each other very much. You can't imagine the jealousies.'

'I *can*. "Restricted information is power." Chapter five of the Simmonds magnum opus. But why do you want to invite this guy round?'

'Oh, I thought it might be interesting to hear what's going on from the inside.'

Nancy could not resist the temptation. 'Chapter three, isn't it?'

'What is?'

'"Inside information provides a thrill of exclusive privilege and excites a sense of superiority".'

'Actually it's "encourages" not "excites", but I am truly flattered at having such an attentive reader.'

'If you remember, my darling, I have typed the darn thing three times. And for your information, you did change "encourages" to "excites" in the second draft.'

John pretended to cower into his corner of the sofa. 'Can I retire to my kennel now?'

Nancy was happy to see a glimpse of his usual self. It made her realize that with hypochondriacs, cosseting only encouraged self-pity. 'So is it *dîner en famille* or is your diplomat friend very formal?'

'I don't really know, to tell you the truth. I never knew him well . . . but yes, I suppose he did strike me as a bit traditional. You know, clean-cut captain of games, hero-worship from the lower fourth and all that. Perhaps a bit too decent for the world he's ended up in. But then you never can tell. Nobody puts the boot in with such convincing public-spiritedness as the British ruling class.'

'The this-hurts-me-more-than-it-hurts-you syndrome?'

'Absolutely. Acquired at Charterhouse in his case.'

She smiled and sighed at the same time. 'Knowing how fanciful you can get, I might even start to feel sorry for this guy.'

John was silent for a moment, his mood changed. 'You know, I think I feel sorry for him too, although I can't for the life of me work out why.'

When he arrived at a quarter to nine Rayner apologized for his lateness even though he had rung earlier to warn them. Nancy looked at him closely. He certainly did not appear the boot-putting-in sort. Neither the grey streaks in his fair hair nor the creases round his eyes diminished the hint of vulnerability. His charcoal-grey suit appeared so awkwardly formal in their house that Nancy wondered how to suggest he take off his jacket. After John's remark about the captain of games, she had expected the arrogantly suave Englishness she so detested.

Just after they had sat down with their drinks, Rayner looked at his watch. 'Oh God! I totally forgot to ring my wife when I left the office. She was out when I tried earlier.'

'Well, give her a call now,' Nancy said. 'There's a phone over there. Or do it from our bedroom upstairs.'

'No, here's fine. Sorry to be a bother.' He smiled quickly and went over to the telephone by the door.

From where John and Nancy sat it sounded as if Rayner's wife was furious. They froze in embarrassment, fearing that their disappearance into the kitchen would only make it more obvious. Rayner was half-bent over the telephone with the receiver close to his head in an effort to prevent them hearing. Eventually he said he would ring later, then quickly put down the receiver. John and Nancy pitied him as he returned to his seat trying to compose his expression.

'Sorry about that,' he said. 'She seems to be rather upset at my not going home yet again. I've been having to sleep in the office these past couple of nights.' He took a mouthful of whisky as if it were medicine. 'Not that there's much we can do. It's just a question of being around in case there's a development which might affect one's own group.'

'Well,' John said trying to be cheerful, 'it's sod's law that anything vital comes up just when you've slipped away without warning anybody.' David's smile of agreement was uncomfortable. He remembered only too well his late arrival on the day of the kidnapping.

'You're really great!' Nancy upbraided her husband. 'He's hardly sat down and you try to make him worry about playing truant for a couple of hours.'

Rayner gave a polite laugh. 'No, that's perfectly all right. I left your number here with the duty officer. At this time of night I can get back in less than fifteen minutes. Obviously it's only the time factor which stops me going home.' They nodded brightly for it seemed as if he was trying hard to convince them.

'Well, anyway, you must be starving,' Nancy said quickly. 'So let's go and eat straight away.'

They all stood up. John watched his guest drain his whisky. The ice cubes dislodged themselves in the up-ended glass and slipped down on to his nose. Rayner wiped it with the back of his hand. He laughed on realizing he was observed.

'God, I needed that.'

'I'm not surprised in present circumstances.' But John's automatic reply forced them both to look sombre.

As soon as they had settled themselves at the table, John looked across at their guest. 'So things aren't going well?' he asked bluntly. Nancy glanced at him, then went back to ladling the soup with a preoccupied air. She passed David a bowl. He smiled his thanks, grateful for a breathing space before facing John. Political advisers did not have much of a security clearance. He also recalled John's comment during the hospital visit that hiring a chariot slave to remind the PM of his mortality did not seem to work.

'Pretty depressing,' David finally replied, gazing at his soup. He took his spoon, then put it down on seeing that his hostess had not yet served herself.

'What? Too many rival empires involved?' John persisted. Nancy looked sharply at her husband. She found him difficult to understand at times. Here he was, completely impervious to someone else's reluctance to talk, yet he hated asking strangers the way and was intimidated by waiters in restaurants.

'There's a bit of that sort of thing, I suppose.'

'Well, you must all be working flat out, anyway,' Nancy put in. Rayner agreed with a smile. Then, in a further attempt to save him from John's pestering, Nancy went on to ask if he and his wife had any children. David looked uneasy. 'No, none,' he replied, addressing himself to his soup. 'Susie was never very keen on the idea.'

Nancy was furious with herself. She felt a fool especially since it was such a stock wifely question. John glared sideways at her, more irritated by her diversion than by the gaffe. 'Oh, yes,' he said taking over again. 'What happened in the end about the curry theory?'

Rayner gave an embarrassed laugh. 'This is such delicious soup that I'm sure you don't want to remember that.' But John explained in a caustic tone to Nancy how a sample of the bodyguard's regurgitated take-away was seized upon for analysis.

'Well,' Rayner said as his host leant across the table to pour him some wine, 'We've heard nothing more.'

'Perhaps the police are keeping a great state secret to themselves. I mean, take that po-faced character who came to see me from your lot.'

'Oh, Sykes. A great systems man is our Commander Sykes.'

'That sounds like the one. I bet he's the sort who hates autumn because the dead leaves are untidy. But I must say, he struck me most as one of those immensely respectable surburban types, who are secretly into bondage and fladge.'

Nancy shrugged to David. 'His fantasy gets the better of him rather often.'

'That's right,' John snapped, astonishing them both. 'You can now blame it on my having been bashed over the head.' They both stared at him confounded by the change of mood. Nancy was alarmed remembering the doctor's warning. She tried desperately to think of another subject. 'I mean it's simply not safe in the streets any more,' John stated with mystifying sarcasm, then stopped to gaze at the table as if another thought had struck him. Not knowing what to say, they watched him twiddle his wine glass by the stem. But then he began to speak, and Nancy immediately recognized the self-searching tone he assumed in lectures.

John launched straight into his pet theory of the 'dictatorship of the consumer durable'. When he finally raised his head to look at them, Nancy sensed with enormous relief that he had not cracked, although his behaviour was stranger than usual. She pondered the doctor's comments on the effect which irrational guilt might produce. David, on the other hand, was still wondering whether they should pretend to take him seriously.

'Forgive my little discourse,' John said, pushing back his hair. 'Strangely enough, it was sparked off by my putting on a record just before you arrived. I couldn't help thinking that the twins are virtually being forced to grow up either hating music or loving it.'

'I don't get you,' Nancy said.

'False absolutes. The way we're pushed, consciously or unconsciously, into a Hobson's choice. An illusion of free will.' He stopped playing with his glass, then pushed it away as if it was a cigarette he was rejecting. 'This morning at Downing Street I found myself staring down at the crowd outside. I despised them, and I despised myself for feeling that way. Obviously I agreed with their concern,' he added lamely, then hurried on to describe the press photographer and the flowers. 'You see, the crowd angered me because they had allowed themselves to become just parrots of the tabloids. It made me start to wonder how much freer we really are than, say, in Russia. That's all.'

'But you're not seriously trying to equate them?' Rayner demanded pushing forward his plate. John insisted that he wanted only to compare, which was not the same thing. Nancy noticed their guest glance covertly at his watch. 'Do you have to be back by a particular time?' she asked, taking the opportunity to stop the discussion before it developed into an argument.

'No, it's not that,' Rayner smiled quickly. 'But would you mind if we watched the Home Secretary's broadcast? It should be starting at any moment.'

'Sure. We can take the fruit through with us.' They pushed back their chairs. John bent to scrape the excess butter from his side plate with a knife. In mild surprise Rayner watched him return it to the terracotta bowl.

The voice of the Home Secretary could be heard a moment before his face appeared on the screen. Rayner's mouth twitched in annoyance at having missed part of it. 'The terrorists' demands', the Home Secretary said, 'include the unconditional release and pardon of convicted murderers in Ulster. It is probably no exaggeration to say that since the Second World War we have never been faced with such a stark choice, such a bitter choice. But to accede to such blackmail would sanction lawless violence. There is therefore no way that Her Majesty's Government can even consider such a course of action.' The Home Secretary's head moved, signalling a slight change of tone.

'With both humility and pride, I can claim to be an old friend as well as political colleague of the Prime Minister. Our association goes back nearly fifteen years, so I think I can say I know him well. I was therefore not surprised some eighteen months ago when, during Cabinet discussions on ministerial security, he insisted that if he was ever kidnapped by terrorists, no concessions should be made under any circumstances. His characteristically brave lead was followed by Cabinet agreeing unanimously that the same would apply for any minister.'

There was a long silence after John switched off the television.

'A bit predictable in the circumstances, I suppose,' Rayner hazarded.

'Very predictable, I'd have said.' John's tone was bitter. 'I'm only surprised they didn't fade out to the Death March from Saul. It must be a real relief not having to worry about leaving him in the lurch. Meanwhile they can all get a nice warm glow praising his heroic sacrifice.'

'That's the only bit of sympathy you've expressed for the man since he was taken,' Nancy observed quietly.

'Don't start giving me any of that guilt syndrome the doctors dished out.'

'Listen,' Rayner reacted angrily. 'I know you've just come through a bad experience and all that. But that gives you no right to imply what you did a moment ago. Okay, there'll always be certain jealousies between departments. That's the nature of the security game. But there are no grounds for saying that he's being abandoned. I suppose you're trying to make out that some ministers are relieved to have him out of the way so that they stand a chance in the next elections. Well, I can promise you from my position on the inside that there's not the slightest hint of any group failing to pull its weight. And it was no act the way the Home Secretary gave us such a rough ride this morning. These terrorists aren't idiots. And the search simply cannot cover millions of houses, even if we used the whole blasted Army. So for God's sake give the security forces a chance instead of making snide remarks.'

'All right then,' John fired back, hardly waiting for him to finish. 'But if the PM's not being abandoned, instead of spouting all that sub-Churchillian crap promising other people's blood, sweat and tears, why in hell didn't he keep open some channel for discussion with the terrorists to give you lot time to find out where they are? He's just slammed the door . . . Or rather the lid of the coffin.'

9

Sykes grunted to himself when the door of his office opened. He was not well-disposed towards Thurston, who had been seconded to the Security Services Liaison Group from Special Branch. On his first day at SESLIG Thurston had revealed himself to be a football fanatic. The requirements of man management had forced Sykes to show a polite interest, but this necessity lapsed with the crisis.

'Sorry I'm late back, chief.' Thurston had been left in no doubt that his superior did not appreciate being addressed as 'guv'. He stood inside the doorway waiting for a reaction. It was hardly as if they could do much except wait by telephones, so he refused to feel guilty at over-staying his first visit home since the flap had started.

'Did you get some sleep all right?' Sykes inquired automatically.

'Crashed straight out after I'd eaten. And to think, the wife was already complaining I used the house like a motorway services.' Thurston gave one of his sharp laughs which grated so much on Sykes's nerves. 'Anyway, the food's about the same standard.'

Sykes quickly turned the subject to work. 'Well, you haven't missed much in the last twelve hours. The Commissioner and the Home Secretary are coming to the view that if there's no advance in the next couple of days, then a cordon and search operation must be prepared.'

'Suppose it had to come. We've got to be seen to be doing something. Reckon it could work, sir?'

'Frankly, I think it is dangerous, even though I have every sympathy with the Commissioner's dilemma.'

'Dangerous in what way? That they'll slip through the net?'

'Not so much that. The only realistic hope of such an operation is to flush the terrorists from cover. But it could also panic them into murdering the Prime Minister.'

The telephone started to ring. As Sykes leant forward to pick up the receiver he nodded a signal of dismissal to his assistant. It was Rayner of the Allied Liaison Group, who wanted to see him. Sykes thought he could guess what it was about.

David Rayner arrived a few moments later. Sykes observed his face carefully while he took a chair. To his surprise, he noticed that Rayner was in a bad temper and made no effort to conceal it.

'Yes, David,' he said noticing how the first name still sounded unnatural.

Rayner sat leaning forward with his elbows on his knees. He rubbed the palms of his hands back and forth against each other a few times, but it was not a gesture of enthusiasm. He looked up, oblivious to Sykes's quizzical expression. 'You remember when we talked about the *Verfassungsschutz*?'

'Yes. The "technical problem" in the DISPOL computer network.'

'*Sabotage*, as you rightly pointed out,' Rayner said, nettled by the reply. 'Your contact in the Federal Police was quick.'

Sykes suddenly understood why Rayner was in such a mood. He was furious at having to admit that his liaison counterpart in an allied service was withholding information. Sykes's face remained impassive. 'You've presumably been told the extent of the damage.'

'Like hell I have,' Rayner snapped. 'Apparently there's a complete clampdown until the internal investigation is completed. Of course they're very apologetic and so on at such an unprecedented move, but that's no bloody help to anybody.'

Sykes took time to reply. 'So I suppose you're hoping for the information via my contact in the Federal Police at Wiesbaden?'

'But don't you see how important it is?' Rayner

exclaimed in frustration. 'The timing is one hell of a coincidence. And if we were to know – '

'Which entries had been destroyed?'

'Well, obviously. It might be some sort of a guide at least.'

'You know, I really don't think that a computer programmer who's been clever enough to infiltrate the West German security service would unwittingly help us that much.' Sykes paused to reflect, then sighed to indicate a difficult decision. 'To be perfectly frank, David, I have in fact heard from Wiesbaden already. My conversation was completely off the record and confidential.' He paused to glance at Rayner, who stared back in amazement. 'The damage is in the PIOS part of their computer system, and it is extremely serious affecting entries on all extremists, both left and right. Much of the information can of course be reconstituted from other systems and traditional files. But it will be some time before they can assess the permanent data loss accurately.'

'Jesus,' Rayner muttered. The seriousness of what he had just heard overshadowed any resentment at having had to come to Sykes for the information. He shrugged despondently at the policeman on the other side of the desk. 'Well, it doesn't look as if there's much we can do then. Except wait for this cordon and search operation . . . which'll have all the finesse of a suburban pheasant shoot, if that roadblock exercise was anything to go by.'

Sykes did not betray any reaction to Rayner's choice of imagery. 'David, I am just as concerned as you. And I also have strong misgivings about the wisdom of cordon and search in this case. But the overall picture may not be entirely black. In fact I was going to give you a ring when I had a moment.'

'What about?'

'It appears that your former colleagues from south of the river have come up with a couple of faces and supposedly matching identities.' Sykes cleared his throat as he passed over two photographs with a few typed details fastened across the bottom with paper clips. 'As you will see, one of them is apparently German. And with the computer sabotage in Cologne, it would certainly look as if some sort of German link is on the cards. But we *must not* allow ourselves to become fixated with preconceptions or hasty theories.'

Once again Rayner stared at the policeman in his functional grey suit. Ye gods, he thought. One day somebody is going to wring that pudgy neck. Then John Simmonds's unsettling remarks of the night before came back to him. Rayner started to wonder with deep unease at the way the Prime Minister seemed doomed through procrastination. But the way Sykes had not bothered to inform him earlier of this development made him even angrier. The police officer remained unmoved by his protest, and his explanation of other urgent matters was almost insultingly superficial.

Finally realizing that he would receive little satisfaction, Rayner picked up the photographs and left Sykes's office. He felt capable of digesting the new development only when back behind his own desk. It was impossible to know whether Sykes had good reasons for doubting the information which the Friends had obtained, or whether he was still afraid of following a false lead. But above all Rayner was preoccupied with the lack of urgency to inform his group. He sensed that Sykes's attitude indicated a mere lip-service to allied liaison procedures. Probably most of the Department and the West German police had been informed first. Sykes had not concerned himself with any polite fiction about the supposed key role of the Allied Liaison Group.

Never before had it occurred to Rayner that his section was perhaps little more than a cosmetic creation to make the Departmental organigram look impressive. And who could be more appropriate for the non-job of fronting such a non-group than himself? Rayner suspected that Sykes just tolerated him like a poor relation – or even worse, like a passed-over dilettante.

10

'So my discreet hero has finally returned,' Susie called from upstairs on hearing the front door. Her voice immediately rekindled Rayner's bad mood. He chucked the car-keys on to the art deco table she had bought without consulting him.

Rayner looked through at the mess in the sitting-room. Only one light was on and the air smelt stale from unemptied ashtrays. He crossed angrily to open a window then went from one table-lamp to another, reaching under the shades for the switch. Usually he complained about the way she left them all on. A book on the sofa caught his eye. He retraced his steps to see the jacket more clearly. It was Saul Bellow's *Herzog*. Rayner's eyebrows and mouth moved in a reflex that was both doubtful and surprised.

He recrossed the hall to the kitchen. There he found the refrigerator bare of food except for a lettuce which had become slimy on the outside, some butter on a saucer and a plastic container of cottage cheese. The sight was an antidote for hunger. No wonder she stayed so thin. He slammed the door making a tray slide off the top. After the clatter he heard her footsteps on the landing. He went to the sink so as to keep his back to the doorway. There were no clean glasses amongst the chaos on the draining board, so he rinsed out a tumbler. As he filled it from the mixer tap, he sensed her leaning against the doorframe behind him.

'Aren't you still out rescuing your leader single-handed?'

He waited until the drips from the tap had stopped before replying. 'It's good to know that you've actually turned on a radio to know what's going on.'

'Can't you do better than that?'

'All right then, tell me about the busy day you've spent . . . buying food, cleaning the house.' He turned round and leant back against the edge of the sink to observe her reaction. 'Stimulating your intellect, being creative with pottery classes and weaving.'

'We're in Repro-Land. Not bloody Hampstead.' She watched David look down at the floor between them. There was something different about him that evening. He raised his head, regarded her coldly, then walked straight for the doorway forcing her to move aside.

Once in the study, he filled the tumbler with whisky before lowering himself into the old leather armchair he called his sprawler. He began to wonder how he had come to make such a mess of things. Other men could turn to their wives, but his career, having disillusioned her, had become the battleground of their marriage. He thought bitterly how it did not even provide enough to buy a bored acquiescence.

Rayner found himself studying the framed photograph on the table beside him. Taken just before their marriage, it had become an image he could never abandon, although the formal pose was completely untypical of Susie. Her skin had been perfect then, before the excessive sun-bathing dried it making fine lines around the eyes. Under the studio lights the blonde hair gleamed. Susie would have preferred the tawny-streaked fairness of the Mediterranean, and had made a number of attempts to imitate it.

She exalted the Latins and derided the unspontaneous English. *Only an Englishman could wear socks with espadrilles*, was one remark which had stuck in his mind. Rayner glanced over at the cupboard where all her Linguaphone records were stored from the days when she had set out to learn Italian and Greek. Susie could not concentrate for long and of course never bothered with grammar, but somehow she managed to make herself understood while amusing everybody with her mistakes.

To hell with the rules was the basis of her approach to life. And she did not bother to conceal her relish for the role of *enfant terrible*. She always spoke off the top of her head, yet often hit the mark with startling effect. Rayner had never been able to work out how much was fluke and how much intuitive genius. *All right*, she had retorted to a comment of his about her aggressive and haphazard arguing at a dinner party. *So I make a spectacle of myself. But what do you really want? A safe timid boring little wife?* She had quickly recognized the way he despised security while secretly craving it. And although her idea that he loved administrative detail was wrong, she also saw through his superficial decisiveness.

Rayner replaced the photograph. At that age Susie was already an unwitting victim of her own looks. The temptation to rely on them had been too great to resist. Like many others she had opted for undemanding jobs since boyfriends competed to provide entertainment. But the apparent advantages of her position soon proved illusory. Left with little self-discipline, she was equipped to be only an accessory for the men she affected to despise.

He was sure that Susie's resentment had always been fuelled by a compounded mistake. Once vulnerable in that way, she had staked depreciating assets on a man who had turned out to be neither rich nor successful. And then she had not had the courage to cut her losses before it was too late. He turned the glass of whisky round and round in his hands. After the meeting with Sykes, it certainly seemed the right night for post-mortems.

He heard her move around in the drawing-room. Shortly afterwards a needle slid across a record. He winced at the noise. She really should have grown out of her taste for rock music, he thought. Apart from forcing him into the role of prude, she never missed an opportunity to emphasize how old-fashioned he was, with cutting remarks about 'shabby gentility'. Rayner had always understood that to mean people fallen on hard times trying to keep up appearances. But her version seemed to centre on his attachment to his grandfather's shotgun, family silver and some inherited furniture. Of course he had to admit that they would look better in an old house with well-proportioned rooms. But Susie's random purchases appeared ludicrous in such a setting. Woodside Close, or the 'neo-Georgian ghetto' as she called it, had been a last resort after an endless series of disagreements.

Eventually Rayner drained his glass with a calm which he believed had nothing to do with the whisky. As he hauled himself to his feet he told himself that it came from facing the truth.

Susie sat curled up in an armchair flicking through a copy of *Vogue*. It took real training, he thought, to be able to pass the time with such a determined air. He looked pointedly at his watch. 'Well, I suppose I'd better see if they've still got a table at Luigi's, or whatever it calls itself.'

'Going out?' she asked without raising her head. 'Should I pin Union Jacks all over me to show that I'm standing up to be counted?'

His sigh turned into a harsh laugh. When he had first met her this contempt for authority had been attractive. Secretly he rather envied it. But when they were married her behaviour often proved embarrassing. It went much further than a desire to shock. Sometimes policemen and traffic wardens seemed to arouse an incoherent rage in her.

While at the telephone he glanced over a couple of times, but she kept her head down. 'Perhaps loyal citizens are organizing spontaneous demonstrations,' she remarked turning back a page.

'I wouldn't be so scathing if I were you,' he replied. 'Under another regime you might have to go out to work.'

'The old threat of the unknown devil.' Her eyebrows rose in exasperation while her gaze stayed fixed to the magazine in her lap. 'Freeze the mind and activate the emotions. My Repro-Land right or wrong!' She threw down the magazine, forced a yawn, then regarded him.

Rayner leant forward with his elbows on his knees and shook his head slowly to give the impression of a despairing parent. When he looked up again, he ran his hand over the lower part of his face with the gesture she called his razor commercial audition.

'I think you really despise all this too,' Susie started again in a quiet voice. 'But you can't admit it. Not with your background . . . *and* school, with its own little pecking order. As far as I remember you said it was a prefect's privilege to walk around with his jacket unbuttoned. And bolshie little boys who did the same were beaten. For their own good of course, because the system's kept going for them too. You've probably forgotten how you told it when we first went out together. You *enjoyed* making it all sound so ridiculous, and I thought: Great! He's not a stuffed shirt. You could laugh at yourself then. But I've often thought since that it might've been better to have judged by exteriors after all.'

Susie stretched round the lamp for her cigarettes. 'The diplomat as social chameleon,' she murmured to herself. Then she breathed out sharply. 'At times I simply don't know what makes you tick. Oh David, if you'd only give yourself a break.'

11

Having felt his way downstairs, David Rayner steered himself to the front door avoiding indistinct objects in the grey dawn light. While struggling into his oilskin shooting jacket he glanced out of the paned window. Hedges, grass and trees began to take on colour under the streaked horizon. The damp cold air felt refreshing on his face when he opened the door. He stood there for a moment before leaning back against the fibreglass portico to pull on his gumboots.

He tried to tread quietly, but the crunching of the gravel was magnified in the stillness. Once on the dew-soaked grass he walked rapidly, leaving the golf-course boundary on his left. He felt a need to work the early-morning chill out of his limbs as well as distance himself from the house. It seemed the only chance to clear his mind.

It was not Susie's assault on his character which troubled him. The urge to be outside came from waking suddenly out of a vivid dream, evidently prompted by the painful truth about his job. He had found himself back in the Army during National Service. His leaden limbs had refused to climb the scramble net on the assault course while a sergeant instructor shouted: 'You're just a tailor's dummy, Rayner!'

Crossing the field towards the wood, on an impulse he looked back. His snaking track was dark in the silver-grey dew. Against a background of heavy cloud, the new brick houses with their white woodwork were lit by a line of pale sunlight. A clatter of wings from the edge of the wood made him swivel. The shark-like profile of a wood-pigeon rose above the beeches. He smiled, remembering how in his childhood he had imagined them as Mosquito fighter-bombers skimming at tree-top level. Seagulls were obviously Sunderland flying-boats circling watchfully. And with great reluctance, because he hated their oily green blackness, starlings in flight had been Spitfires. Then, for a reason he never managed to pinpoint, he suddenly remembered Simmonds telling him in hospital that the terrorist who attacked him had a dimple in his chin. Rayner stood in the middle of the field amazed at having forgotten such a thing when he looked at Sykes's photographs. He set off back towards the house in a lumbering run.

The dash to London reminded him of when he picked the morning of the kidnap to have it out with Susie. But this time he was propelled by a compulsion to find out more, not by the panic of missing a vital conference. He forced his thoughts away from daydreams of some spectacular coup which would prove everybody's scepticism wrong. Trying to calm himself, he made an effort to concentrate on priorities. He mustn't make a fool of himself by setting off false alarms.

Once in sight of the George and Dragon bas-relief over the main entrance he reached inside his jacket for the plastic pass, remembering Susie's outburst on the subject of identity cards. He left the Lancia in the car park and mounted the low flight of steps in two strides. Inside the hall, he realized he was sweating.

'You're back early, sir,' the front desk commissionaire greeted him. 'Thought you'd've been allowed a lie-in by now. Still, it's all right for some, isn't it?'

Rayner shrugged. 'Life goes on.' He knew that if Susie were there she'd make some sarcastic remark about the modest air of self-sacrifice. Well, damn her, he thought stabbing at the lift button a second time. He was angry with himself for even considering what she might say.

On the third floor, he instinctively turned right out of the lift, but then went back down the corridor in the opposite direction. Sykes's office was dark behind the opaque panels of lined glass. Rayner paused to survey its frontage. There was no doubt it was larger than his own even though ALLIG and SESLIG officially ranked equal on the 'wiring diagram'. Irritated with himself at having bothered to check, he turned away sharply.

Once the strip lighting had flickered on, Rayner unlocked the desk, took out the photographs, and laid them on the blotter. His eyes remained fixed on them while he stood removing his coat. Neither of the two faces could have belonged to the terrorist who attacked John Simmonds. It then struck Rayner that the police would have checked shots of only British and Irish suspects after interviewing him in hospital. At that time there had been little indication of foreign involvement.

The Intelligence Liaison Group's registry downstairs had a photograph for almost every name on the watch lists from allied services. Any chance of stealing a march on Sykes was overwhelmingly attractive. Rayner looked at his watch. Once again, his assistant Nigel Pannet was late. Rayner cursed him, but then decided that he would prefer to do the job himself.

He stopped at the automatic vending machine by the lifts. According to a wag in Sykes's group, the milky-grey coffee had been specially blended to match the carpet tiles for when people seized their throats in disgust. The liquid was so hot that only from above could he hold the rolled lip of the plastic cup.

Down on the first floor at the entrance to INTELLIG, Frances Campbell, the registrar, informed him that neither refreshments nor smoking were allowed in the data area. Her glance in the direction of the security guard by the lift was a clear reproof for having failed to stop him. Rayner inclined his head in apology before retreating to leave the cup on a window ledge.

'You've probably done me a service,' he smiled on his return. 'Everyone says there should be a government health warning on those machines.' She stared back at him as if to say, then why go near them in the first place.

Her ruthless common sense had rapidly achieved an awesome reputation. The head of INTELLIG had predicted wrongly that Rayner would be the only man capable of 'charming the claymore down from her highland crag'. The folder she clasped in one hand was transferred to the other, signalling in office semaphore that she was in a hurry. Her impatience was stressed by the brusque removal of the black-framed spectacles which Rayner thought made her look like the head of a secretarial agency.

'I just wanted to check through European watch list details.'

'How far back do you want to go?' she asked.

'I'm not sure, but I'd have thought at least two years.'

'Well, that should be no problem. Providing you have the time,' she added laconically. She led the way through the swing doors to the registry. 'That German name Commander Sykes gave us yesterday was Bavarian, I think.'

'Oh, do you know the south of Germany well?'

'I spent two years at the university in Munich.' Frances Campbell stopped in front of the bank of filing cabinets, gazing at them reflectively. 'But that's not very relevant to the problem.' She pulled open a drawer. Rayner suppressed a sigh of irritation. He wondered whether she enjoyed her reputation.

'Right,' she said, indicating the sections. 'Watch list details from Cologne, Paris and Rome. Any material you want copied must be signed for. Nothing must leave the room, as you know. Please make sure that it all goes back in order.'

'Well that's enough to keep me occupied for a bit, as you said. Thanks for your help.' She acknowledged with a curt nod before turning to answer the telephone on the desk by the door.

With the files open on top of the cabinets, Rayner turned the quarto-sized cards over one at a time. Each entry consisted of a computer reference serial at the top with a copy of the telexed details stapled across lower down. The majority had a photograph of the subject attached to the top right-hand corner.

It took Rayner a little over an hour to work his way through the last two years of the German section. He suffered a feeling of anti-climax, uncertain whether to go back further, or start on the offerings from the French security service, the DST. He looked at his watch. Pannet had not yet rung down to report his arrival in answer to the message left on his desk, so Rayner went to the telephone to check with his secretary.

With a weary sigh he returned to the cabinets to start on the French entries. After turning the first twenty cards mechanically, Rayner did a double-take. He flicked back the last one to examine the photograph again. The subject, Raul Bloch, had a round dimple in the centre of his chin. Just like Kirk Douglas's, Rayner noticed irrelevantly. The square hard face and clipped hair bore no other similarity to the film star. Rayner's eyes scanned the telex slip eagerly, but a mention of the Foreign Legion made him relax in disappointment. The man was hardly a candidate for the role of Red Vanguard terrorist with an involvement in extreme right-wing groups and a short career as a mercenary in central Africa.

Rayner grunted as he went back to turning the cards. But then a few moments later he decided out of curiosity to check Bloch's birthplace. It was Saarbrücken. A wild theory started a sense of unease within him. Jesus, it can't be, he told himself.

Having checked quickly that Frances Campbell had her back to him, he detached the photograph then slipped it into his pocket. Afterwards, he scribbled down the basic details.

'Any luck?' she called across on noticing him write.

Rayner swivelled guiltily on hearing her voice. 'Oh, no,' he replied with a quick laugh and replaced the file.

'I'm sure Paris can give you a much fuller rundown,' she said eyeing the drawer. He watched guardedly to see if there was a suspicious element in her manner.

'Er, yes, of course. It was just a hunch. I'll contact them if necessary.'

'We're always at your service,' she replied looking at him over the top of her spectacles. Rayner was almost certain of a humorous glimmer in her eyes. A suspicion that she somehow found him amusing had unsettled him once before.

Back in his office Rayner shut the door carefully. He needed privacy to think. Different scenarios featuring Bloch mingled in his head like haphazard sequences in a dream. Rayner told himself to stop this speculation. He needed information, not wild hypotheses springing out of what could easily be mere coincidence.

When Nancy answered the telephone, he quickly thanked her for supper the other evening.

'Oh, you must come again,' she replied, 'now that John's back on form. Not that that always means a quiet life,' she added with a half-laugh. 'Seriously though, David, I'm sorry he gave you such a heavy number.'

Rayner assured her a little too earnestly that he had enjoyed himself. But then sensing he had overdone it, he quickly asked if John were there. Nancy replied that because he had been lying around the house depressed, she had pushed him off to the British Library to research his book. Rayner cursed silently at not having gone down to INTELLIG earlier.

'But listen,' Nancy said. 'He won't be back before six at the earliest, knowing him. So why don't you drop round for a drink, then stay for some food afterwards.'

Rayner insisted that he only needed to see John for two minutes and he did not want to put her to any trouble.

'Okay, suit yourself,' she replied. 'But there'll be food here if you want it.'

While replacing the receiver Rayner thought for an instant of the bare refrigerator at home and regretted his instinctive refusal. He sat staring at the telephone for several moments, dismayed at the prospect of having to wait until the evening. Once again he studied Bloch's face, and began to fear he was expecting too much from John Simmonds.

Nervous tension soon forced him out of the chair to pace around the confines of his office. He stopped suddenly to reach across the desk for his agenda. The next liaison meeting in Paris was due some time during the next fortnight. A date should have been agreed already, but the crisis had thrown routine fixtures to the winds.

Dismissing wariness of an imprudent move, Rayner settled himself quickly at the telephone. Christian Morgan, his counterpart in Paris, did not betray surprise at this sudden request for what was supposedly a low-priority meeting. But Rayner had little difficulty visualizing the expression of faintly amused scepticism at the other end. Morgan was no fool, and so it would be virtually impossible to obtain information without revealing at least the direction of his suspicions.

Rayner's mouth contorted into different shapes as he continued to ponder the problem while gazing blankly at the map of Europe on the wall. He started when Nigel Pannet entered the office to apologize for his lateness, then hurriedly moved his note pad to hide the photograph of Bloch. Pannet did not notice, having immediately launched into an unconvincing diatribe against London Transport.

As often happened, Rayner was at first irritated by Pannet's man-of-the-world act, then almost started to feel sorry for him. The whole performance was not only unnecessary, but achieved entirely the oppposite effect; like the rather brash suits which drew attention to his shortness. To make matters worse Pannet also tried to play the thrusting meritocrat. Rayner felt that he thus bore a certain similarity to the director-general, who apparently longed for a knighthood in spite of his progressive affectations.

'I had a call from Paris,' Rayner said ignoring Pannet's excuses. 'Morgan wants to advance the liaison meeting to tomorrow. So I'm taking the early flight from Gatwick.'

Pannet jerked in his chin to signify surprise. 'But you can't miss vespers.' The Friday-afternoon meeting of group heads was sacrosanct. Rayner swore angrily that it had slipped his mind. 'Got to have the Direktor-Generalissimo's personal dispensation, according to the holy writ on the subject. And I'd've thought he regards it', Pannet slipped into bad mimicry, '"as a not unimportant conference in view of recent events".' He pulled forward a chair and sat in it with one continuous movement. 'If you can't miss the pow-wow, what are you going to do? Ring Morgan back?'

'No. There are good reasons for going tomorrow . . . on both sides.'

'Good enough to risk a distinguished row?'

Rayner cursed him silently for his persistence. Once again he wanted privacy to think things through. 'Yes,' he said with an irritated sigh. 'Good enough in the long term anyway. But for the moment there's nothing for it except a day off sick. So, let's say that unless you hear to the contrary, I will have rung in just after nine to warn you. You attend, so as to brief me later. Okay?'

'But what if they insist on ringing you at home? You never can tell.'

For all his bravado, Rayner thought, he's just another umbrella man ready to ward off any shit flying around. 'All right then,' he said impatiently. 'Tell them I've had a bit of a fall, and the doctor's sent me to have some X- rays done.'

The other inconvenience came at the end of the afternoon when Susie rang from a call-box. He assumed she had been on another of her cinema sprees, going from one film to another. Apparently her purse had been stolen, and she wanted to go back with him. Rayner was highly sceptical. He suspected that she had spent too much or else forgotten to cash a cheque before the banks closed. Angry at her choice of day for such a performance, he told her to meet him at a nearby pub after half-past six.

12

Nancy greeted them at the door with the news that John had only just arrived. As she ushered them through, Rayner's forebodings were increased by Susie's murmur to him: 'Stripped pine and ratatouille?' Such was his conviction that she and the Simmondses would loathe each other on sight, he had attempted to leave her in the car while he showed John the photograph. To his dismay she had insisted on coming in with him. Usually any friends of his were automatically classified as boring.

His heart sank when Nancy felt obliged to repeat her offer of supper and Susie was too quick for him.

'Only if you're absolutely sure it's no trouble. That'd be wonderful as it'll be pretty late by the time we get home.'

In his anger Rayner was tempted to make some reference to the emptiness of their refrigerator. Her acceptance again confirmed his view that Susie was basically a scrounger.

Nancy was also secretly disheartened; John had reacted in a very disgruntled fashion when she warned him that David Rayner would be dropping round. After their speculation on what his wife was like, following the row on the telephone, Nancy eyed Susie frequently while fetching their drinks. Nancy placed her as one of those English girls in the Sixties who had started that occupation of looking after Mediterranean villas and ski chalets. Her skin had a grainy texture like Moroccan leather from too much sunbathing.

Nancy tried to visualize the Rayners when they met some fifteen years or so before. The dream couple in the ads, or rather, pulp fiction, she decided. Good-looking young diplomat woos and acquires beautiful fresh blonde, she thought in a confusion of harshness and pity. The greater the romantic illusion, the crueller the disappointment. It was nothing new. They just represented a particularly striking example. Nancy considered for a moment whether they might have stayed together afraid of admitting that their image had been a mirage. She handed them each a glass of whisky guessing that the Rayner household drank its way through more bottles in a week than they and their guests in a year. Nancy could imagine John complain afterwards on seeing their depleted stock.

'Oh, but David's a creature of habit,' she suddenly heard Susie laugh. It took Nancy a moment to remember that she had asked them a pointless question about travel up to London. With mixed feelings, she heard John's footsteps on the stairs.

Wearing jeans and an old beige sweater, he paused in the doorway as if reluctant to enter the room. His hair was splayed out on his collar like a hood which weighed down his head. Adjusting his spectacles, John gave David a quick smile, then nodded guardedly at Susie as they were introduced.

'So how are things?' John asked turning back to her husband. After Nancy's upbraiding over his behaviour on the previous occasion he made an effort to be cordial.

'Still just waiting at the end of a telephone,' he replied. 'I have to keep ringing in to say where I am.'

'It's like in that Woody Allen film,' Susie put in. 'What was it called?'

'*Play it again, Sam*,' Nancy replied. David smiled quickly. He was nervous that Susie would come out with some bombshell at any moment.

'Anyway,' he said, turning back to John, 'we're just a clearing house, so we can only wait on the actions of others.'

'It looks like a long one,' Susie remarked quietly. David shot her a warning look, which she ignored. 'I'm starting to feel sorry for the newsreaders. It must be difficult thinking up variants on "Still no advance in the hunt for the Prime Minister". But of course it may all be a subtle plot to give the terrorists a false sense of security.'

A silence ensued. John looked at her carefully, then Rayner muttered that her flippancy was hardly in good taste.

'Well, darling, I must be consistent. After all I am the only member of the bad-taste club in Repro-Land.'

With arch tolerance, David explained her term to the uninitiated, but he was put out to find John enthusiastic about it. Nancy knew her husband's thought processes only too well.

'If I were you,' she warned Susie, 'I'd copyright it before he starts getting plagiaristic ideas like Repro-Democracy.'

Susie then went on to make them laugh by describing the golf-club dance and the neighbours in Woodside Close. Rayner was torn between a certain relief that the Simmondses seemed to like her, and annoyance at her dramatic exaggerations.

During the move towards the kitchen, he seized his chance when John stayed to collect the glasses. 'You remember telling me in hospital about the one who hit you? The one whose chin you noticed.' John looked at him almost suspiciously before nodding. Rayner brought out the photograph of Bloch which he had been fingering in the side pocket of his suit jacket. 'Do you think this could be the man?' he asked, and then waited impatiently while John studied it.

Eventually he lifted his head only to make a grimace of uncertainty. 'I suppose it could be. But obviously you can't identify someone after seeing him for a split second.'

'Yet you wouldn't rule this face out,' David persisted.

John examined the photograph once more with reluctance. 'No, I wouldn't rule him out. So that doesn't even help a process of elimination. Who is this character anyway?' Rayner was saved by Nancy calling through to them. He murmured something about a suspected member of Red Vanguard.

After the Rayners had left, Nancy flopped down next to her husband on the sofa. 'Well, well, well,' she teased him. 'And who said he was going to be bored to death?'

John gave a defensive shrug. 'It's a funny feeling to like somebody you know you should disapprove of.'

'I began to think you'd really fallen for her. Honestly, you were just like an excited teenager at one point.'

He leant over to kiss her neck. 'Ah gets these foony spells, yer know.'

'It's all very well playing the fool, but you should have bothered to check David's reaction. The longer you two went on laughing, the angrier he became. I thought we were about to have a nasty scene.'

'Oh?' he reacted with innocent surprise. Nancy was exasperated to find that she could not be sure he was joking. 'But what makes a woman like that tick?' he asked, ignoring what she had said. 'I can hardly see her indulging in Hausfrau masturbation . . . cleaning and dusting the whole time. So is it some form of apathy from feeling she's left it all too late?' He suddenly noticed her expression. 'What the hell are you smiling at?'

'It's always a temptation to underestimate those you want to feel sorry for, just as much as those you resent.'

13

Rayner shivered with early-morning tiredness. A gust of wind across the car park blew his hair into his eyes as he bent to lock the door. Coke cans rattled emptily over the concrete surfaces. He loathed Gatwick. It was still a package-holiday airport to him even in October.

The strongest impression of the place was a lack of permanence. At times the terminal appeared to be little more than a network of Portakabins. There was always work in progress with diversions round scaffolding or hardboard partitions. And in the almost deserted main hall the white box counters increased the building's resemblance to a child's construction kit.

With his *loden* over one shoulder and briefcase in the opposite hand, he stood in the short queue at the check-in desk. The whirr and click of the automatic departures board updating itself make him look up. His flight was shown without any notified delay, so he did not bother to listen to the announcer. At less than thirty minutes from the time he left home, he had to concede that the whole process was far less disagreeable than he made out.

Rayner felt light-headed and weak in the legs after little sleep, as he always did when taking an early flight. But what disturbed him was the way he could not seem to concentrate on the immediate problem. He had relapsed into the mechanics of getting himself to his destination, instead of working out how to convince Morgan that his interest in Bloch was of no significance.

He walked over to buy a copy of *The Times*. The paper-boy had not come by the time he left the house. He glanced at the headlines of the others. With no concrete developments in the hunt, the press had to concentrate on the implementation of the new security procedures. Rayner turned away slowly.

Walking towards passport control, he wondered how the computerized system had progressed. He saw little sign of it when the immigration officer looked at the photograph before raising his eyes to compare it with the face. Rayner knew that they learned that movement of studied casualness on their basic training course. But then he noticed a small visual display unit and keyboard with loose flexes in one of the unoccupied booths. It looked as if the programme would be operational very soon. SESLIG had claimed it would take less than four seconds to obtain a complete reading on the screen from the time the first figure of the passport number was tapped out. Rayner continued along the expanse of purple carpet which led to the duty-free area. He decided to buy Morgan a bottle of malt whisky.

Rayner had always suspected that the ostentatious futurism of the Charles de Gaulle airport at Roissy with its moving walkways in plastic tubes represented the summit of the French love-hate relationship with the United States. This strain of aggressive modernity dated from the late 1960s when they had suddenly started to compete with what they had despised. Still, he thought, only the French would install voice-modulation devices on the announcement systems to make the girls' voices sound sexy. However, he found such artifice far more attractive than Gatwick's atmosphere of British Rail sandwiches.

On the ground floor of the huge concrete rotunda Rayner's eyes searched for the blue-and-white sign indicating the Roissy rail-link to Paris. Around him the business men seemed shorter than in England. And in more of a hurry as they swallowed cups of coffee at the refreshment counters without even casting an eye over a folded newspaper.

Despite the unhappy memories of Susie's disillusionment with diplomatic life when he was a second secretary there,

Rayner refused to let go of the early moments together. Paris had always excited him. Whiffs of caporal tobacco smoke in the warm stale air of the Gare du Nord convinced him he was back more than the voices and noise around him. Yet he had always remembered the city by smells like roasting coffee, damp stone, garlic, street markets, wine and traces of scent in the pavement bustle. With little difficulty he could shut out the posters and the radio commercials of monotonous enthusiasm. He also managed to ignore the modern constructions which besieged the old centre. They were part of another city, with no more interest than downtown Chicago, Düsseldorf or Milan. Still less did he want to acknowledge the new satellite towns which disfigured the Île de France countryside with high-rise blocks and shopping complexes designed as the hearts of artificial communities.

In the taxi the German shepherd dog on the front passenger-seat raised its head. The driver stroked it, assuring Rayner that the animal was *très gentil*. Rayner made a doubtful expression. He suspected that an Algerian would be told the opposite. Considering the obsession in New York for exotic pets, he was surprised that cab drivers there did not drive around with wolves or boa constrictors. When Rayner gave the address, he observed that he was carefully examined in the rear-view mirror. Rayner smiled at the memory of his embarrassment the first time he took a taxi to Century House in Lambeth. He had not known how to react when the cabbie joked: 'Is it now 003½ with the cuts, guv?' Rayner settled himself in the corner, out of the driver's vision, to watch the streets.

Christian Morgan came down to sign him in at the front desk. They shook hands and ran through the usual polite exchanges on their way up in the lift. Morgan's office was a cramped but high-ceilinged room with a single window which gave on to the courtyard below. The walls were white and the fittings different tones of grey. The filing cabinets were exactly the same shade as those of the British civil service. Rayner thought that perhaps some world-wide colour standard had been established for the ubiquitous symbol of the bureaucrat international.

He wondered how Morgan with his sophisticated tastes could stand it. But then he was a strange fellow to have joined the police in the first place. All those who knew him well had speculated on his motives. Most favoured the theory that he enjoyed both a wry interest in human vices and the intellectual challenge of a complex game. Rayner assumed that Morgan could hardly be satisfied with his present job, unless content to observe the infighting with amused cynicism. The rivalries within the French security organizations made the resistance of their British equivalents to a centralized liaison network appear a model of co-operation.

Rayner guessed that Morgan must be at least five years younger than himself, which he found slightly unsettling. Morgan was tall with floppy black hair which he often brushed, back with a languid gesture. Morgan's background was unmistakably the *grande bourgeoisie*. And when his flippancy was not apparent, he seemed to carry the *ENArch* mandarins' air of effortless ambition. Appropriately he had spent a couple of years at an American university, though Rayner could not remember which one.

Before they sat down Morgan went to give his secretary some change for the coffee machine. Rayner placed the bottle of malt wrapped in its plastic carrier bag upright on the desk. On his return Morgan raised his eyebrows in appreciation. '*On boit un coup maintenant?*' Rayner smiled, shaking his head. Morgan bent to slide the bottle into the bottom drawer of the desk.

They settled themselves with their coffee; mercifully, not a symbol of international bureaucracy, Rayner observed to himself. There was a short silence as each waited for the other to begin. Morgan tilted his head. '*Messieurs les Anglais, tirez les premiers*,' he said with an indecipherable smile. 'But if you have nothing of particular urgency, can we not put liaison business on a back burner until I have heard the inside story of the last few days?'

Rayner rearranged himself in his chair. 'As you'd no doubt guessed, Christian, I thought we could kill a couple of birds with one stone by this meeting. Well, three in fact. Brief you personally.' He paused to acknowledge Morgan's grave nod. 'Compare our liaison status reports. And check out one suspect with you.'

'Certainly, David. In whatever order you prefer.'

He would almost have felt easier if Morgan had immediately asked who it was. But telling himself to avoid coyness, Rayner tackled the question of Bloch directly.

'Listen, shall we first of all sort out this identification problem?'

'By all means.'

'Well, as you've no doubt heard, we haven't yet got a firm lead on the terrorists.'

'The computer "problem" in Germany has not helped, so I've heard.'

'Er, quite. We have, however, received one rather dubious lead. Now, the description resembles that of a certain Raul Bloch who appeared on your watch list ten months ago. But according to your people, he's an extreme right-winger, so the Red Vanguard connection is improbable, to put it mildly. In any case our informant only saw a portion of his face for a split second.' Rayner gave an unconvincing shrug. 'It's a flyer we've got to check out, if only for the purposes of elimination.'

Morgan refrained from pointing out that this procedure was usually accomplished by telex. He looked up from playing with his pen. 'I think I recognize the name, but I cannot of course remember the details. Do you have the watch list reference? It would save time.' Rayner gave it to him. Morgan pushed himself up from the desk. 'I will ask somebody to fetch his file and obtain the latest sighting information from *Renseignements Généraux*. It should not take long.'

When he returned Morgan looked at his watch before sitting down again. 'Are you staying in Paris for the weekend?'

'No,' Rayner replied in surprise. 'I'm booked on the five o'clock flight back. Why do you ask?'

'Friday meetings are convenient for weekend travel,' he answered with an amused look. Rayner relaxed, remembering the occasions on which he had rescheduled meetings in the past. This time the possibility had not occurred to him. He had even forgotten that the weekend was upon them. Then he was reminded of the group heads' gathering from which he was playing truant. What an idiot, he thought. The chief's not going to believe it wasn't just for a weekend in Paris.

'It will take them about ten minutes to have a reply from *Renseignements Généraux*,' Morgan added. 'Shall we start on the liaison reports now? I have booked a table for one o'clock. Perhaps you would tell me then about the great hunt. You British now seem to be as good at saving hostages as you are at organizing royal ceremonies.'

Rayner was taken aback by such an inappropriate comparison. It reminded him of the bad jokes made by Susie the night before. Until that moment he had managed to forget the row on the way home. While Morgan flicked through his copy of the liaison report Rayner became aware of how hot he felt. He regretted having put on a waistcoat that morning. French offices were always stifling. Leaning forward in his chair to unstick his shirt he saw Morgan looking at him expectantly.

When the file on Bloch arrived Morgan asked if he minded him refreshing his memory first. Rayner replied with an expansive gesture which he then suspected had been overdone. He pretended to study the calendar on the wall above the desk. Eventually Morgan pursed his mouth before handing the file across the desk. Rayner took it with a dip of his head in acknowledgment. Hiding his eagerness required a considerable effort.

The biographical notes contained few surprises. Two years after Bloch's birth in Saarbrücken, his father had been imprisoned by the Allies for a short time during the process of de-Nazification. Aged seventeen, Raul Bloch enlisted in the Foreign Legion armoured regiment. Rayner skimmed through discharge, suspected OAS involvement, and membership of the European New Order movement in the late 1970s.

'Twenty-third fiddle in the Black Orchestra,' Morgan commented dismissively.

Rayner nodded without looking up. But then controlling his reaction on spotting one entry, he raised his head. 'I see what you mean. But tell me, what's this "case officer X-14" bit?'

'Oh that. Bloch was evidently used as a body by "*La Piscine*". All these fascist *voyous* are from time to time.' Although Morgan's disclaimer was probably true, Rayner was jolted by this direct link with the SDECE, the French equivalent of the Friends. The Swimming Pool nickname came from the closeness of their headquarters to the public baths in the Boulevard Mortier. 'I would not read too much into that,' Morgan added. 'You know how *retro* those provincial aristos who run the Swimming Pool are. Clean-ups or not, they will still go on employing such people to beat up the Left *pour la patrie et la gloire*.'

Rayner knew that Morgan claimed proudly to have never voted in his life out of a disdain for politics of all varieties. But he was still shaken by such indifference.

'Anyway,' Morgan went on, 'it's not just the lifeguards from the Swimming Pool, as you know. There are quite a number in the police as well. Links with Italian neo-fascists were shown after the Bologna station massacre. But to go back to Bloch. He was probably just used as a messenger boy under . . . the old pals' act.' Rayner confirmed the phrase with a quick nod. 'So probably "X-14", or whatever he calls himself, was an officer who knew him in the Army. It's an incestuous little circuit. Like in other countries.' Morgan studied Rayner's expression with a wry smile. 'I hope all this does not shock you, David. I know you have spent time in France, but you must not forget our history. Rather than admit to incompetent leadership, there is an element in French society which has a dramatic taste for conjuring up traitors. We adore good scandals,' he said with an irresponsible wave of his hand. 'You British appoint Royal Commissions because you have more respect for secrecy. Or perhaps you are more embarrassed about revealing the hypocrisy of rulers.'

'Christian, I'm surprised that *you* should subscribe to the "Major Thompson" school of English studies.' The irritation in Rayner's retort was provoked more by the way they were leaving the point than in defence of the English character. In an emphatic manner he studied the file once more, but his brain did not seem to absorb what his eyes focused upon with so much effort. His imagination was racing with confused possibilities.

'When was Bloch last sighted?' he asked suddenly. Morgan, who had been tipping back his chair, let it fall forward with a thud. He checked the sheet he had been given. 'A week before the watch list date. Seen in Strasbourg.'

'And why exactly was he included on the watch list if he was the petty ruffian you make out?'

'Oh, I suppose nowadays *Renseignements Généraux* and the DST feel that a bit of tokenism is called for.'

'What on earth do you mean by that?'

'Why, including any spare right-wing extremists of course. Then they can't be so easily accused of political bias. According to the *fiche* Bloch was only wanted for having fire-bombed an empty synagogue three years before.'

Rayner swallowed at the cynicism, despite having believed Morgan could not shock him any more. He opened his mouth to remind him that Bloch had been employed by a sister service, but he fell silent. There was little point unless he wanted to see yet another variation on the casual shrug or the eyebrow-raising act. Morgan regarded him closely, but Rayner just shook his head to tell him not to worry. He even assumed it would do no good to criticize such an attitude to the watch list on his return to London. His job specification emphasized that ALLIG's prime objective was to foster co-operation, not to put backs up.

'Hungry?' Morgan inquired. Rayner said he was, although the emptiness in his stomach had little to do with appetite. 'I thought that this time', Morgan said, 'I should take you to Chez Alphonse.' Rayner muttered that he was sure it would be excellent. Evidently Morgan had a similar emphasis on the importance of international liaison written into his job specification. And, knowing Christian, he had probably passed an underlined copy to the accounts department.

'Do you want to leave your case here?' Morgan asked. 'I will be locking the office.' Rayner agreed, watching him secure the file on Bloch in his desk. Rayner's mind still dwelt on the question of watch lists and their distribution amongst allied services. Willi's group in Cologne naturally received copies like the rest of them. And the West German procedure was virtually identical. Immediate namecheck through the computer and updates where necessary before onward distribution to the different security services.

Rayner's thoughts went back to the discussion in Sykes's office. The policeman had told him quite plainly that the entries eradicated from the PIOS computer system included both left- *and right*-wing extremists. Rayner experienced a sensation in his guts like the after-effect of a punch. But noticing Morgan's inquisitive look, he forced a smile and said that he had forgotten something important. Could he ring his assistant in London?

'But certainly. The white telephone is an outside line. You know the *indicatif*, don't you?'

To his relief Morgan left the room to give him privacy. Rayner felt weak as he dialled Cologne to arrange an urgent meeting with Willi Afflerbach.

14

After buckling his seat-belt Rayner tried to recall the Lufthansa advertisement. As far as he could remember Air France offered style, the British promised care for their passengers, the Americans a lavishly insincere welcome, while the Germans just stated that their aircraft ran on time. The remorseless economy of the cabin staff's smiles certainly seemed to emphasize their priority of virtues. Such an attitude usually made him feel uncomfortable, but this time he welcomed it.

Pushing up the plastic blind, he peered out of the window, which was streaked with rain. Under the low evening cloud, lights glistened on the wet tarmac. He craned his neck for any sign of imminent departure like the ground crew giving a thumbs-up, or vehicles driving away. Having spotted nothing to give him hope, he raised himself awkwardly in his seat to look over the rows of headrests. There was little indication that the door at the front of the aircraft was about to be closed, even though all the passengers were seated. The air hostess was chatting to the cabin steward. They're just the same as the other bloody airlines, Rayner fumed.

His anger masked his anxiety. For the whole afternoon, the interminable lunch during which he had constantly wanted to go to the lavatory, the return to Morgan's office to finish the liaison evaluation report, and the long wait at the airport for the flight to Cologne, Rayner had kept telling himself he must be crazy. Exaggerating a dimple on a German thug's chin into a great neo-fascist conspiracy. What was Morgan's phrase? Twenty-third fiddle in the Black Orchestra. But now, on board the aircraft, he felt that much more committed, and so tried to banish his tenuous suspicions. There may be damn all to go on, he told himself, but there's no denying the whole thing's got a weird feel. Somehow it was like going round a wall to find that the mirror you had been looking at was two-way.

Rayner shifted restlessly in his seat. He could not help thinking about the cover-up of the crisis in September 1968. Following the Soviet invasion of Czechoslovakia several divisions of the *Bundeswehr* suddenly moved up to the East German border without warning. Senior hard-liners in the West German army had decided that the moment for national re-unification had arrived, with the Warsaw Pact forces bogged down and demoralized there. Few of their NATO colleagues had dared admit the current level of support for the neo-Nazi party amongst *Bundeswehr* regulars.

Uneasy speculation grew while senior NATO commanders warned their West German counterparts that allied forces would have no option but to pull back across the Rhine. A cousin of Rayner's in a Guards regiment later recounted the atmosphere that evening at the Royal Dragoons' dance for the Lippspringe polo weekend. He had described it as the Duchess of Richmond's ball before Waterloo, only in reverse. *Honestly, lad, we were all asking if we'd have to shoot the nags and stick the regimental silver on Three Tonners before dashing back to the Belgian frontier.*

Ordering their unit commanders to destroy the sealed orders in red envelopes, the *Bundeswehr* generals pulled their troops back before dawn. The Bonn government managed to retire most of the senior officers involved in this secret fiasco. Then soon afterwards the hard Right's electoral support seemed to collapse, so nobody worried any more. The whole episode was only remembered now in NATO circles as just one of several trigger points during the Cold War.

'Lufthansa regrets to announce that there will be a twenty-minute . . .'

'Blast!' Rayner cursed between clenched teeth. The businessman in the aisle seat lowered his copy of *Die Welt*, gave him a laconic smile, then returned to his article. God, it was bad enough hauling Willi out on a Friday evening, let alone making him hang around. What was his wife's name? Trude? Ilse? Something predictable, anyway. He half-remembered a healthy fair face, although he might be imagining her as a female version of her husband. There had been a framed photograph in Willi's office which he had once studied politely. Several children were shown ranged on either side of her in front of a house. Both Willi and his wife were Catholic, he recalled from some remark about church taxes. Counter-spooks always seemed to be either believers or out and out atheists. But then as one doubtful example after another came to mind, he rejected the generalization, irritated at the way his concentration was wandering.

Rayner tried to force his thoughts back to the so-called Black Orchestra. Morgan's remarkably dismissive view of the neo-fascists even made him consider whether it was an attempt to put him off the scent. Hell, he muttered to himself, I'm going to go crazy if I start doubting everyone.

That fear of wild suspicion was familiar. A reminder of that first inkling of Susie's affair echoed back a sickly sensation. He laughed harshly against himself. The city of love was really the city of betrayal. Not only did it happen in Paris, he thought, struck by a greater irony, but in certain ways Susie's lover had resembled Morgan. 'Lover' was of course a grossly cosmetic description, he reminded himself in a habitual attempt to diminish that memory of inward writhing, speared by humiliation. Even now his memory-clips brought hot resentment in the wake of pain.

Rayner felt he had tried hard to understand her motives, but he still did not know whether she had wanted to shock him and gain attention, or was just after an illicit thrill. In calmer times he felt sure that her lunchtime sessions had been no more than that Parisian ritual which embellished convenient opportunities for passing lust. So convenient that Susie became bored once the affair was no longer a secret.

With a sudden flurry of well-practised actions, the cabin staff prepared for take-off. Rayner sighed in relief, then tried to concentrate again on the dilemma of how frank he could afford to be with his other allied counterpart.

Willi Afflerbach was waiting for him at passport control. He wore a dark-green polo neck and the sort of tweed jacket which continentals believe to be typically British. His barley-coloured hair was neatly cut as his solid features seemed to require. Not too Aryan, Rayner had thought when they first met. In fact the very model of a modern German democrat.

Once they had set off across the arrivals hall, they began to inquire after each other's wife with guarded formality. Willi's English, like Morgan's, carried an American inflection. An unspoken protocol existed amongst the allied liaison officers whereby the visitor's language was always used. During their fitful exchange Rayner glanced at a brightly-lit sex shop by the arrivals hall. Might be amusing to buy Susie something really grotesque, he thought. Especially after her bad-taste-club thing. But she'd just wait for an uncomfortable pause at a dinner party, and then tell everybody. He could almost hear her: 'I was thinking of wearing it tonight, but I thought that black leather was really a little too "Come-as-you-are".'

Rayner was about to comment on the sex shops, but remembered Willi's impatience. Light remarks would not be appreciated after pushing the panic button.

Nothing was said as they walked rapidly together along the neon-lit corridor, only separating to overtake family groups and their trollies piled with luggage. In the car park Willi indicated a new Audi. Forgetting he was no longer in England, Rayner headed for the wrong side, and grinned a quick apology.

Willi switched on the engine to warm the car, but made no preparation to drive away. He prompted his passenger with an expectant look, then pretended to study the instrument panel.

'First of all,' Rayner began, 'I'm sorry to mess up the start of your weekend.' Noticing the tense way in which Willi fingered the thick black steering-wheel, he hurried on. 'What I mean to say is that all this may turn out to be a wild-goose chase. It could just be a strange coincidence, but I have a nasty feeling about the real identity of the terrorists.' Willi breathed out of the corners of his mouth. Rayner understood this to signify that it was what he too had secretly feared. 'So before going any further, I assume you haven't had any joy checking out the details we've passed you so far.'

Still staring at the instrument panel Willi shook his head. 'Not a thing. It was quite a task I am telling you. We have name-checked all aliases, but the mugshots do not match known political activists.'

'Right as well as left?' Rayner insisted quietly, pulling his briefcase up on to his lap to search inside for the photograph. 'He may be one of them. Raul Bloch. Born Saarbrücken 1943.' Willi flicked on the interior light for a moment to study the face. 'All I'm saying', Rayner continued in a controlled voice, 'is that others in Red Vanguard might also belong to what Christian calls the Black Orchestra.' He paused so as to emphasize his next point. 'Now, does that make the sabotage of PIOS entries on both left *and right* a little more explicable in your view? Or unlike some European security services, can you be sure that neither the *Verfassungsschutz* nor the Federal Police contains neo-Nazi sympathizers who might help by sabotaging a computer or two?'

'Of course, nobody can be sure,' Willi replied with an edge of irritation. He handed back the photograph.

'Anyway, you'll agree that the possibility of Red Vanguard being a destabilization attempt at least needs checking out.'

Evidently preoccupied, Willi inclined his head in acknowledgment. 'How did you come by this theory?'

Rayner gave a short laugh. He had just remembered Christian's theory on the balance of intrigue. It would probably have been more amusing to somebody in the right mood. Rayner apologized on seeing Willi's unenthusiastic expression. 'It just seemed as if everyone's got a theory except me.' He then hurried on to outline how he had come to Bloch.

When he had finished Willi's mouth twisted down sceptically. 'As you say, it's a real shaky connection. Besides, who the hell do you think . . .'

'There's no point speculating, Willi, when we can see if a few facts check out or not.' Willi again moved his head in acknowledgment, though this time the gesture was noticeably more reluctant.

Bearers of uncomfortable tidings are never popular, Rayner told himself. The inside of the car was becoming fugged up, so he wound down his window a little. Willi shook his head as if to warn him against disappointment.

When they reached the slip road leading from the car park on to the main route out of the airport, Willi said that perhaps it would be better if he went alone to the Innere Kanalstrasse. He seemed relieved that he did not have to look at his passenger. Restlessly he checked the rear-view mirror, the handbrake and the gauges on the dashboard.

'Whatever you think best,' Rayner replied after a few moments. 'What do you want to do? Drop me at a hotel just beforehand?'

'No. You're very welcome to stay the night with us.' There was evidently little warmth in the invitation, yet Rayner made only a half-hearted attempt to protest.

Cocooned in the Audi they drove fast in virtual silence down the autobahn. Pairs of red tail-lights curved into the distance. Rayner made a comment about the weekend traffic and Willi grunted in agreement. Several times they had to slow suddenly because of patches of autumn fog.

'So how was Christian?' Willi eventually asked after easing his weight from one buttock to the other.

'Oh, the same as usual. Well, more cynical than ever, if that's possible.' Willi had never really hidden his disapproval of the Frenchman. Rayner suspected that Morgan had mocked him too cleverly on some occasion, and besides, the motives of a dilettante, however professional, aroused suspicions in anyone with Willi's thoroughness. Rayner went on to recount the casual admission over the watch list. Willi did not appear shocked, it just seemed to confirm an opinion. Even at their first meeting he had commented on the Latin obsession with corridor politics. Rayner remembered the remark mainly because he had never seriously considered France a Latin country.

As soon as they turned from the main road into a complex of suburban streets Rayner guessed they had arrived. Willi's fluid turns of the steering-wheel as he leant with the corners showed that he could follow this part of the route almost blindfold. Rayner looked out at the parked cars under the streetlights and the neat grass rectangles sloping up to the sort of houses whose red-tiled roofs made them look like children's building sets. It was a damp hazy night and Rayner felt refreshed by the air after the overheated car.

'Please,' Willi said, indicating that he should go first. Rayner smiled quickly and set off up the path of perfect crazy-paving. Willi reached round him to open the front door, then once again gestured him forward. Having found himself starting to imagine Susie's comments, Rayner tried to ignore the oak door with its black iron studs in a medieval style.

Evidently Willi's wife had heard them, for she stood ready in the main room looking as if she had just tidied herself. Like her husband, she had a healthy complexion and was solidly built, though not fat. Rayner glanced round the room, the centre of which was lit by a fake cartwheel chandelier. Below it stood a heavy round table in dark wood which one of them had probably inherited. A Renaissance shape chair in the form of a curved X made of dull steel and leather was positioned by the large brick fireplace. Neo-Teutonic, Rayner could not resist commenting to himself. But at least there weren't any reproduction swords hanging on the wall.

In contrast to the sombre pieces there was a small bar in the far corner with an illuminated aquarium, a low sofa in tan suede of over-comfortable design, and a bright Alpine landscape. The mixture of Spartan and indulgent was very German, Rayner thought.

Two little boys with neatly brushed blond hair, wearing slippers, pyjamas and dressing gowns, shuffled self-consciously into position from the opposite doorway like a recruit guard of honour.

'David,' Willi said suddenly making an effort to welcome him. 'You have not met my wife, Ingrid.' Rayner shook hands with her, saying in German what a pleasure it was after hearing so much about her.

'Please, can we speak in English?' she asked. 'It is so good practice for me.'

'Of course,' he replied, guessing she was a wife determined to be an asset to her husband's career. He wondered fleetingly if Willi told her anything about his work, but somehow it seemed almost like wondering what they got up to in bed. Secrecy and intimacy didn't go together, as they emphasized on the security course.

Ingrid called the two children forward to say good night. Rayner squatted to shake their hands, then Willi took them off to bed. Ingrid asked him whether he would like a drink first, or a wash. Rayner took the opportunity to apologize for the trouble to which she was being put, but all the time he was asking himself why Willi did not want to take him to the Innere Kanalstrasse.

'And do you wish to telephone your wife?'

'Perhaps I could do that first,' he said smiling his thanks.

'Please. Of course.'

She left him alone after pointing out the telephone on the bar. Having dialled, he found himself studying the two ugly brass candlesticks on the brick mantelpiece. Susie's first comment was bound to be something along the lines of 'How jetset you are, my darling.' He started to believe she must be out, it took so long to answer. She laughed when he explained where he was, but did not make the remark he expected. 'Just a joke against myself,' she explained. 'By the way, I've asked John and Nancy Simmonds to lunch on Sunday, kids and all.'

'And they're coming?'

'There's no need to sound so amazed. Yes, they are.' Slightly taken aback, Rayner could only say that he hoped to return by the end of the morning. He sensed that she was about to add something but decided against it. As he replaced the receiver he shrugged, unconvinced. Then he went off in search of his hosts.

'Ingrid will look after you,' Willi told him. 'Are you hungry?'

'Not after Christian's lunch, thanks.' Willi did not smile back. He just said that, in that case, they would have something together when he returned.

After Rayner had washed, he joined Ingrid in the sitting-room. She rose to pour him a drink at the bar. Their conversation followed a predictable course of polite disinterest. He asked how long they had lived in the house, and about the children. During this exchange his mind was preoccupied with the information that Willi would bring back. But after several minutes of their contrived time-killing he sensed that she was uneasy. Rayner was sure it did not come from shyness or uncertainty over her English. His presence made her uncomfortable. He could only assume that she somehow believed he represented a threat to Willi. Perhaps she had become hypersensitive because she could do no more than speculate on the basis of her husband's moods. Ever since the computer sabotage, she must have known there were problems, even if Willi had never mentioned it.

'Does Willi tell you anything about his work?' he asked her on a sudden impulse. Ingrid stiffened as if he were trying to trap her into an indiscretion. 'No, it is not allowed.'

'Well, of course, it's the same for us. I was only trying to say how difficult it must be for you at times like this, when you know he's involved with events in the news.' He forced a smile, willing her to relax. 'I don't have that problem because my wife doesn't seem to be very interested.'

He sensed immediately that she did not believe him. How could a wife not take an interest? For her it was probably an incomprehensible dereliction of duty. Rayner was not surprised when she asked a few minutes later if he would like to watch television.

As soon as Willi returned, Ingrid disappeared to the kitchen. 'You have everything you want?' he asked Rayner, who assured him that his wife had been a marvellous hostess. 'She is putting out a cold supper for the two of us. She ate with the children earlier.'

Rayner made a suitably appreciative reply although disturbed by the way the programme seemed almost pre-arranged. Perhaps the warning conveyed in his telephone call from Paris had been more obvious than he thought. Reluctant to prompt, Rayner noticed how Willi busied himself with the details of hospitality. All the time his eyes managed to avoid Rayner's face. Willi's manner implied that he did not want to be drawn until he could make a full statement without distractions.

Rayner's impatience became almost unbearable as he waited until the ham, cheese and salad had been laid out on the round table. Ingrid eventually took her leave of them, but even then Willi occupied himself opening a bottle of wine with slow deliberate movements.

'Willi, I don't want to appear rude,' Rayner said, unable to contain himself any longer. 'But what did you find out?'

Again he avoided Rayner's eyes while pouring the wine and passing plates across the table to urge his guest to help himself. Finally he looked up.

'I found nothing. There was no trace of Bloch on the computer.'

'Okay, but then we know that both right and left entries had been sabotaged.' Rayner waited for a reply but Willi remained silent. 'So what about the conventional filing system?'

'There is no file.'

Rayner gave a disbelieving laugh. 'But just like the rest of us, your procedure means that a file is automatically opened on any watch list subject. And Bloch appeared on a watch list, whatever rating you give to burning a synagogue.'

'Yes.'

'But I gave you the watch list reference. Surely, that's on file isn't it?'

'Yes.'

'So what's the deduction? Has whoever's responsible for starting the file made a slip up? Or has it been deliberately destroyed?'

'Neither.' Willi rearranged his plate. 'Bloch's name does not appear on our copy.'

Rayner sat there shaking his head in frustrated bewilderment. 'Christ, Willi, you don't exactly seem to be bending over backwards to get to the bottom of this one.'

Willi pushed his chair back, then walked over to the bar in the corner. He stood staring at the angel fish in the aquarium. Rayner wondered whether his criticism had gone too far, but he was still amazed by Willi's reluctance.

'David, don't you think it would be better for you to be on firmer ground before continuing with this theory?'

'What do you mean? That I should have answers before asking questions? That's a Catch-22 if ever I heard one. Or do you mean by "firmer" that I should be sure of official blessing first?'

The partial satisfaction Rayner achieved from his riposte was cut short when Willi turned round with a distressed expression. Rayner instantly recognized it as that of a man suffering from a conflict of loyalties. There was no doubt about which would win. The welfare of his family went with not rocking the boat. Pension, salary, home, social standing, all were at risk. Who'd employ an ex-security man, if the Federal Government said he wasn't to be trusted.

His earlier unease at the evening's development tightened into sudden suspicion. Christ, he must have reported to higher authority as soon as I telephoned. And maybe he was told to invite me home in order to keep me under observation. For the first time Rayner felt afraid.

15

The idea of pigeon shooting in the wood had occurred to Rayner in the bustle of Cologne-Bonn airport during the wait for his flight back to London. His urge was for fresh air and the chance to think in the open as much as for the encompassing ritual. Not having been out with the gun for a long time, the prospect was all the more attractive. Concerned that the farmer who owned the land might not be in later, he had rung Susie asking her to telephone him immediately.

Game bag, gun and cartridge belt lay ready just inside the front door. Susie stood leaning with her shoulder against the wall as he pulled on his green rubber boots. 'Somehow I feel I should be hanging on to a mastiff straining at the leash.'

Rayner could not resist smiling back. He was surprised that she was in such a good mood, and yet at the same time it seemed so natural. 'I hardly see a mastiff being much good for pigeons,' he said standing up straight.

'Oh, you're so boring,' she sighed. 'I suppose it should be a labrador slobbering amiably over everyone in sight.'

He grinned quickly while struggling into his oilskin jacket with the corduroy collar, then leant over to give her a kiss.

'Well, well,' she remarked. 'Is this the head of the family sets forth to feed his dependents routine? Or are you turned on by bloodlust and excited by the smell of leather and gun oil?'

He laughed and said that he was bound to miss, even if there was anything around. 'Well, if you do astound yourself, my modest darling,' she replied, 'just don't expect me to pluck and gut. All right?'

Having crossed the field, Rayner took up position on the edge of the wood. He breathed in the air of damp leaves and earth, and listened to the wind rattle the branches above him. Further into the wood the creaking of a pine reminded him how earlier in the year a similar noise had proved to be the multiple rap of a wood-pecker.

He gazed back the way he had come at the neat uniformity of Woodside Close. On the far left of the line, smoke from a bonfire was blown around by gusts. He was certain he caught the smell at one moment, but there was no further trace when he sniffed rapidly several times. With the wind in his face he decided to move. The pigeons would turn in to land against it on the other side of the wood. In the distance he heard the raucous double cry of a cock pheasant. It was a sound which never failed to thrill him.

Seeking to understand his exhilaration, he ignored a subconscious warning that this could also make it vanish like a pleasant dream. The contrast of his surroundings to Cologne and the office was so great that their threat no longer seemed real. The only doubt came when he recognized that it resembled that false sense of security in a car speeding through fog patches, like last night on the autobahn.

A chain saw was jerk-started into life at the far end of the wood. Rayner cursed, wondering if it would scare off the pigeons as well as disturb the peace. But a few minutes later he heard the swish of wings. He swung sharply bringing the gun up into his shoulder. As the wood-pigeon veered on spotting the movement, Rayner pulled at the trigger, but it did not give. He took an instant to realize that he had forgotten the safety catch. 'Get organized, you twit,' he said aloud.

Not wanting his good humour to dissipate, he thought of Susie teasing him in the hall just before he left the house. That was what had made him feel so different. That was how their marriage had been at the beginning before her split personality created such difficulties.

Rayner suddenly envied the stability of Willi's home life, however dull and claustrophobic. Everyone needed someone they could trust when it was time to run for cover. He wanted Susie now, but defences could not be lowered easily after the recent sniping. The process had become ingrained with compulsive reactions – jab first to protect your own weaknesses. It made the raw spots fester. He had been wrong the day before. He should have said Paris, the city that corrupts trust. Loneliness in a double bed.

Standing under the tree with the gun sloped on his shoulder, Rayner brought it down to hold with both hands, then smiled faintly to himself wondering whether the movement could be interpreted as Freudian. For some reason he found himself remembering Goethe's reference to the old German belief that cuckoos turned into birds of prey for the winter.

Rayner found it difficult to accept that the bitter arguments were a recent development. Even when forced by Susie to concede, he still convinced himself that their move to the country was the occasion, not the cause. Deep down he knew he had probably gone about it the wrong way. His brother's decision to sell the family house in Somerset after their mother died had provoked a desperate need in him to have somewhere in the country, but two homes would have been far too expensive. What riled him the most was Susie's argument that they had ended up with the worst of both worlds. She of course had never really wanted to move from London in the first place.

The slightest reminder of Somerset provoked in him a nostalgic longing. He never could forgive his brother. David had been given first refusal, but since it was obvious he could not afford to keep it up or commute from there, that had only exasperated him more. There was now virtually nothing left of that world. Not surprisingly, Susie argued that such attachments were an emotional vulnerability, not a strength. He grunted, remembering that the only thing she seemed to like from his past was the photograph of his prep school Cricket XI where he sat in front, cross-legged with brushed fair hair and his head slightly tilted. Anyway, he thought unloading the gun, Susie was now about all he had left. It seemed ironic that she should have become his past.

16

Susie had been brought up in Essex by her mother. She could not remember her father, a young sapper officer who was killed clearing a minefield after the war. Her elder sister Janet tended to take charge more and more. Their mother, never able to cope well, began to indulge in self-pity when her second husband left after only two years of marriage.

Susie did not share Janet's dreams of finding the right man. As a result of the way their step-father had lusted after her, Susie had fewer illusions. When just seventeen, she was expelled from Fulton Grange, the girl's public school to which she and her sister had been sent. Susie called it Dothegirls Hall. The low quality of its teaching was only surpassed by the crassness of its social aspirations. 'It wouldn't have happened if I'd gone to the local grammar,' was her sole justification on arrival home. Janet thought that she had wrecked her whole future. Susie told her not to be ridiculous and walked out of the room in anger.

She returned soon afterwards to announce her intention to live in London. She would get in touch with their uncle Gerald who was seldom mentioned because of his homosexuality. 'Otherwise I'll find a job in Woolworth's,' she added defiantly. Then to shut out the storm of protests, she barricaded herself in the sitting-room and telephoned her uncle.

Contrary to the convictions of both her headmistress and sister, Susie had not been to bed with a boy. She remained chaste for her first year in London, despite a barrage of propositions. The approaches only managed to irritate her. On one occasion when she did go back with a man to his flat after dinner, she suddenly reacted against the routine. Walking out while he was in the bathroom, she caught a taxi home. The man arrived at her uncle's house near Notting Hill Gate just after her. She was thankful that Gerald was away because the man hammered at the door calling her a slut and a whore.

Susie started a secretarial course, which her uncle paid for, but left after a quarrel with the principal over time-keeping. Susie still managed to find a job with a firm which rented villas in Italy. She lied about her qualifications, but luckily little typing and no shorthand were needed. Her passion for the Mediterranean developed that year when she spent a holiday with her uncle on Corfu. There she made love for the first time, having chosen a Greek boy even younger than herself, who came to sit by them on the beach one afternoon. Her uncle tactfully restrained his own interest. Susie felt a great sense of release on losing her virginity, but the boy proposed marriage with deadly seriousness. The idea of female tourists as sexual cannon fodder had not yet permeated Mediterranean youth.

She felt restless after her return to London. She went out a lot and to bed with several men until she became irritated with the pointlessness of it all. For the first time since leaving, she went back to Essex for a weekend, but Janet's complacency and her mother's platitudes uttered with such profound conviction became too much to bear.

On the point of giving up her job to find work abroad, Susie met a rock-music promoter at a party. Paul claimed to have been a barrow boy and to have made his money by spraying sparrows yellow for sale as canaries. It was the period when Society and the pop scene circled each other with mutual fascination in such places as the Club del Arethusa. Susie was dazzled by the famous names and faces. Suburban Essex, eat your heart out, she thought triumphantly, when she moved in with Paul. She felt very sophisticated as she flirted with drugs, although she would not touch heroin after seeing its effect on one of

Paul's acquaintances. Her language and behaviour became even more outrageous. Paul's circle egged her on, particularly after she pretended that her school had really been a convent.

With great reluctance, Paul eventually allowed her to accompany him on a visit to his family. Susie was very disappointed to find that they did not live in the picturesque poverty which she had been encouraged to visualize. Paul's jealousies and roughness, which until then, she had ascribed entirely to his background, now started to make her think more carefully. Some weeks later when a party after a gig deteriorated, Paul punched her for playing around with a drummer, although Susie's action had been no more than a response to the casual infidelities which he saw as natural.

Leaving behind the Mini and the clothes he had given her, Susie went back to her uncle's house. Five days later Paul arrived, truculent yet contrite. Wanting to believe him, Susie returned to his flat, but another violent outburst in the spring convinced her that she would be better out of it. Visualizing the two of them and their friends ten years on made her decision surprisingly easy.

Although the scene, which once had so excited her, now only repelled her, Susie felt dejected by the lack of alternatives. The predictable reactions of her mother and sister kept her away from Essex, in spite of a loneliness which was increased by Gerald's absence. Eventually she rang him at Cagnes in the South of France where he was staying with old friends. She was told to come down and her morale revived immediately.

The amusing conversation there seemed so stimulating in comparison to what she had just left, that Susie was extremely susceptible when a young diplomat was brought over to lunch by friends living nearby. After his looks, the first thing which impressed her was his flawless French. Although no linguist herself, the toneless plodding of an English accent made her squirm. She also discovered that he spoke Italian and German as well.

David Rayner seemed able to behave as an equal amongst much older people as he quipped with them and added to the scandalous anecdotes about famous characters on the Riviera during the Thirties. Paradise for Susie was no longer the Rolling Stones blaring from an open E-Type Jaguar on the King's Road. Suddenly it had become wine, good conversation and laughter abroad. An expatriate life appeared infinitely preferable to anything she had experienced before.

Amused at the sudden change in her, Gerald planned a dinner for his hosts at a restaurant to which David Rayner was also invited. Susie joked in embarrassment about his matchmaking. Gerald teased in return about the conversion of St Susie. Having loathed Paul, he made no attempt to conceal his pleasure. But then it looked as if nothing would come of his efforts on her behalf. David Rayner returned to London unexpectedly, and a week later Susie had to do the same on hearing that otherwise she would lose her job. The holiday romance that never was, she thought fatalistically, knowing the time had not been wasted. She had experienced a short period of happiness which had also satisfied her. The days of casual kicks were really over, she swore.

The company still fired her, and so on the urging of the girl with whom she found a flat, Susie had some test shots done for modelling. She set off on the round of photographers and advertising agencies with her portfolio. The assumptions of many people she saw made her furious. To one photographer's assistant, she said: 'I don't fuck anyone for a job, least of all you!' The insulting situations she found herself in made her think even more of Cagnes. Remembering the conversations there and her own limited contributions, she blamed herself for having messed around so much in the past. She was determined to stop going out and start educating herself instead. But her desperate attempts to concentrate on the philosophy books she bought seemed hopeless.

In yet another of her reactions, Susie felt a need to escape, to 'freak out'. Encouraged by her flatmate, she began to start leading a wild life again. But then she stopped just as suddenly. 'What the hell am I doing?' she demanded in amazement. Her flatmate shrugged.

A few days later her uncle telephoned to say that David Rayner had just been in touch to discover her whereabouts. Susie was delighted at Gerald's teasing. Several seconds after she replaced the receiver, the telephone rang again. Susie had to stop herself laughing during her attempt to sound surprised. David would not have been able to guess that it came from nervous relief and happiness.

However fortunate the timing, Susie's healthy disrespect for romantic fiction did not allow him to appear as a saviour knight in her imagination. She tried to dismiss the question of his looks, telling herself that she just liked his conversation and humour in comparison to the other men she had known in London. David Rayner did not strive to impress her as they had in their attempts at instant seduction. Susie started to feel a strong affection for him when his eyes flickered sideways at crucial moments. Cosmopolitan assurance could no longer hide a *pudeur anglaise*.

When Susie led him off to bed two weeks later, she felt pleased at the way she had handled things for them both. The pace had been perfect, she thought, then laughed at the way that made it sound like a cricket match. Susie could not of course suppress her outrageous side. It fascinated David. Her nerve made him envy the freedom it seemed to represent. Meanwhile she imagined his freedom through languages, travel and, above all, his qualifications. She had only the haziest understanding of what his job involved.

The question of marriage began to hang over their relationship uncomfortably. In conversation they hurried on whenever one of them happened to mention the future, without thinking. Susie tried hard to keep her mind off the subject. Not because she thought that might prevent it coming true. She just feared that discussing it would send everything back and forth inside her mind – a crazy swingball of pros and cons. She confided to Gerald that the idea of 'the relations scene' requiring best behaviour and an inane fixed grin made her feel like 'a Trappist monk about to be press-ganged for a chat show'. Gerald could not help laughing. It was almost as amusing, he told her, as the time she came back from Paul's parents furiously disappointed that they were not proper working-class. Although Gerald genuinely sympathized with her dilemma, he also knew the difficulty of offering Susie advice. 'So what'll you do when the issue does raise its ugly head?' he asked.

'I'll say, yes, of course. I want him. But that still doesn't stop me wondering whether the whole thing's totally nuts.'

To Susie's surprise and relief, David also wanted a quick quiet wedding. She never quite made out the relationship he had with his family. When he eventually took her down to Somerset for a weekend, she found that her visions of gushing in-laws had been far from the mark. David's family amazed her with their detachment. The undemonstrative behaviour made her think of partners in an old firm of solicitors. She wondered if the elder brother in Hong Kong was the same. On arrival Susie had thought that she was evidently the sort of girl that mothers didn't want their sons to marry. Later while helping David's sister pick raspberries in the garden, she asked if there had been some other girl with whom her parents had hoped David would settle down. The sister looked at her in surprise, then understood. 'Oh, goodness no. Their only fear was that he'd marry somebody frightfully boring, or else rather bossy and much older. No, I think they quite like you.'

Susie recounted this exchange to Gerald after the weekend, but he thought that it must be another of her little embellishments. The two of them were very alike in that way.

Later she thought that somehow the atmosphere of the house in Somerset had infected her subtly. At times she found herself regarding the whole question of marriage as a problem of personal administration to be resolved. David was soon to be posted to the Paris embassy. 'Part of what's called the Elizabeth Arden circuit,' he explained with a slightly self-deprecating smile. 'You know, Rome-Paris-New York.' He had found a flat in the Latin Quarter, on one of his official trips, which he wanted her to see as quickly as possible. She was thrilled at the area, having feared deathly respectability in the 16th or Neuilly. When he started to explain rather laboriously about her application for a *Permis de Sejour*, Susie suddenly asked whether she needed to know how to cook properly. She burst into laughter at his surprised expression. 'Couldn't I give them my Spanish omelette? And for starters we could always fill doggy-bags with those goodies they hand out at the receptions.' Not entirely convinced that she was just joking, David's smile was cautious.

Susie loved Paris when they began living there in September. 'It's so much better in the autumn than that old cliché of the spring,' she told her uncle on the telephone trying to persuade him to come over for a long weekend. 'You could spend all day in the Café de Flore ogling the boys.'

'How depressing that would be.' Gerald had become very preoccupied with his age. He was deeply affected by the suicide of a past boyfriend.

Susie did not wait to throw herself into sight-seeing and exhibitions. Leave something for later, David advised her with amusement, but Susie was into Culture in a big way. She would recount everything she saw with ingenuous enthusiasm, although still always the first to laugh at her own mistakes. The funniest howlers she would repeat at parties. In bed after one such occasion, David murmured that without her he'd probably be a very boring person.

Early in the new year several of the senior wives felt that it was time Susie was put right on certain matters. At an informal dinner she had said that it was 'bloody ridiculous not being allowed to take jobs'. Then at an Indian embassy reception she had congratulated the Cuban Chargé d'Affaires for unusually imaginative compliments by kissing him on both cheeks. She did not care that only two days previously HMG had delivered a note of protest to Havana.

Susie arrived for tea with the Naval Attaché's wife and guessed that the assembly of chief hens signified trouble. Susie tried to rein in her temper, but the regal condescension of the minister's wife and her hostess's statement that in the diplomatic service 'one is married to a career more than a man', became too much for her. 'Would I be spared that if we got divorced and just lived together?'

About the same time Head of Chancellery took David on one side for a private word. Fearing that reproaches might prompt Susie to much greater folly, he said nothing to her afterwards. Meanwhile, convinced that David would become furious with the chief hens if she told him what they had said, Susie also decided to remain silent.

Despite David's advice to stick to tonic water alone, Susie became slightly drunk at another reception a few weeks later. Her behaviour was noticeable but not scandalous. David felt that he now had to mention the Head of Chancellery's informal warning. Susie was almost left speechless by the shock of finding that basically he agreed with the chief hens' views.

As Susie recognized later, it was unlucky timing to have met François so soon afterwards. And it was such a banal pick-up. She had dropped her shopping in the street, he helped her to collect it, then proposed a drink at the café opposite. His black humour and irresponsible cynicism were refreshingly attractive at that moment. A real cad, she told Gerald on the telephone, you'd like him. She ignored her uncle's warning. Ever since her childhood in Essex, any feeling that the world was against her provoked her even more.

François claimed to be a scriptwriter, but Susie never took that seriously. They were free to meet any weekday since he had no office to go to, and they bothered with few precautions against being seen together. One day Susie had to do a sharp about-turn in the street on recognizing the Naval Attaché's wife. During lunch François insisted that they spent the afternoon making love in her apartment as a change. Susie's scruples were dulled by the wine she had drunk. So after François returned from the lavatories downstairs, they took a taxi straight there.

Three-quarters of an hour later, when they were lying in bed smoking cigarettes, Susie heard the lift stop at their floor. 'Oh shit, this is bad drama,' was her first thought before the reality of the situation sank in. When David opened the bedroom door François just stared back at him with an enigmatic smile. David demanded who the hell he was. François gave a look of mock surprise. 'I thought the only thing an English gentleman asked his wife's lover was whether he took soda or water in his whisky.' Susie thought that David was going to attack him. Naked, she moved between them, telling François to get out. He said nothing more.

In the silence following François's departure Susie waited for David to speak. 'Well,' she said hesitantly, 'that was a fair cop.' It was all she could think of in the circumstances.

'I didn't know,' he replied in a hoarse voice.

'What on earth do you mean?' But one look at his face told her he was speaking the truth. 'Then what were you doing coming home now?'

He sighed heavily still avoiding her gaze. 'Someone rang the switchboard and told them to pass me a message that you were very ill at home. I dialled here immediately . . .' he paused, then with his head he indicated the telephone off the hook by the bed. 'All I got was the engaged tone.' Still avoiding her eyes, he went to the kitchen for a glass of water.

'That fucking cow!' Susie breathed to herself. She grabbed her clothes, put them on hurriedly, seized her handbag then disappeared out of the front door. In the taxi she prayed bitterly that the Naval Attaché's wife would have a full complement of senior wives to tea. She was not disappointed.

That night David sat staring across the street at the *oeil de boeuf* window opposite. Susie watched him from the corner not knowing what to say. The childish frustration at not being able to turn the clock back had passed. Apparently it could not have been the Naval Attaché's wife who phoned the switchboard. David had been summoned by Head of Chancellery and the harsh terms for his continued employment were spelt out. That evening Susie appreciated for the first time how much becoming an ambassador some day had meant to him. She was sure that he felt a desperate need to make his family sit up and take notice of him.

'I really seem to have loused it all up for you. Don't I?' Without shifting his gaze he nodded. 'What do you want me to do?' she asked. 'Pack and get out? Shoot myself? Lock myself up for ever in a convent? Just say.'

He managed to raise a sad smile.

17

'Have the Sunday papers arrived yet?' David Rayner called down over the bannisters.

'They're on the table in the hall.'

Glancing at a front-page article about another night of rioting in the Midlands, he wandered to the kitchen. In the doorway he halted, staring with astonishment at the scene. Every worktop was covered with bowls and kitchen equipment. He had totally forgotten the lunch which Susie had arranged in his absence. Feeling that she had virtually appropriated the Simmondses behind his back, he instinctively took an aloof attitude.

'There's coffee in the Thermos,' she said, carefully weighing out flour, having checked in a cookbook held open with a carving knife across the pages. The protracted shuffling around behind her back started to get on her nerves. 'What are you looking for now?' she demanded as she bent to take out a Pyrex dish. Glancing up at him her eyebrows rose at the sight of his shooting jacket over pyjamas. For a moment she was tempted to comment how attached he seemed to have become to it. 'The sugar bowl's in the cupboard where it usually is,' she said quietly.

'All right, I'll leave you in peace, now.'

David went slowly through to the main room holding the mug steady. He chucked the papers on the sofa before dropping down beside them. He yawned, patting his mouth with a hand like a stage Red Indian. In between sips of coffee he checked the box which advertised the special features. He put his mug down then pulled open the paper with a jerk to fold it back down the middle. The three-page feature began with a reconstruction of events since the Prime Minister's abduction.

The previous Sunday the newspapers had devoted pages to the ambush with photographs and diagrams of the Pimlico junction. This week the shortage of hard news was disguised by general articles such as résumés of the Moro and Schleyer kidnappings, summaries of international reactions and assessments of terrorist activity over the last ten years. The first one he looked at carried a carefully-worded piece criticizing the security services for having been caught evidently unprepared. Rayner gave a scornful grunt. Only two months before they had published an article on surveillance and the Big Brother State.

Its rival, on the other hand, avoided criticism of the police and Five. Instead it concentrated on welcoming the emergency measures, especially the reintroduction of capital punishment for any terrorist action which resulted in loss of life. The paper's major article, entitled 'The Threat to Democracy', covered the renewed rioting over unemployment and the kidnapping in apocalyptic terms.

Rayner grimaced and put down the paper so as to finish his coffee before it went cold. His most immediate worry centred on the director-general's reaction to his absence on Friday. Immediately after arriving back from Germany Rayner had rung the duty officer, only to be told that there were no messages for him but to keep the switchboard updated at all times with his current whereabouts.

Despite leaving instructions for Pannet to ring him, he had not managed to make contact. Rayner quickly looked at his watch, then went to the telephone on the other side of the room. The noise of the mixer in the kitchen assured him that Susie could not overhear, so he dialled Pannet's home number. He ran his hand nervously over the stubble round his mouth.

'Nigel?' he asked as soon as the receiver was picked up.

'Yes, chief.'

'Am I disturbing you?'

'She's in the bath if that's what you mean. How was Cologne?' Rayner had a sick sensation in his stomach. 'How the hell did you know I went there?'

'The great white leader's Man Friday rang down at close of play. Asked about liaison meetings with Morgan *and Willi*. Very tricky it was after my heart-rending account of your gammy leg. You're to see the great man at ten tomorrow. At least you won't have to keep remembering to limp.'

'You mean I just need to have both arms up ready to ward off what's going to fly in my direction. Oh, Christ!' He groaned. 'Sorry, it's not your fault. But didn't he say any more, like where he got his information from?'

'You must be joking. I think his tone might best be described as "abrupt and unforthcoming". Anyway, you're probably in the best position to work out who did tell him.'

'Okay then, but what about the meeting? Has anything fresh come up?'

'Not officially. The Yard's been bypassing us, not that that's any great surprise, and going straight to their chums in the Federal Police at Wiesbaden. Jungle drums hint that identification of the terrs is in the wind, but they're certainly not letting us in on it.'

'But is this part of the same whisper which the Friends heard?'

'Sykes was asked that in the meeting, but he just trotted out some PC Plod cliché about investigations being pursued. By the way, his lot seem to have had a sniff of your gadding about as well. That joker in SESLIG asked me with a smirk across his face what vital evidence Lord Peter "Whimsey" was bringing back from his secret mission.' There was a hint of malicious satisfaction in Pannet's tone.

'That's all I bloody well needed.'

'Just keeping you briefed.'

It seemed to require a surprising effort to replace the receiver. Rayner sat there not knowing whether he was past caring or devastated. With a sudden wave of empathy he understood Willi's anxiety in a way he had never appreciated at the time. Rayner felt in a confused way that not only had the assumptions and attitudes of his whole career become twisted up, but the material base of his private life as well. He now despised the rather supercilious way he had imagined Willi's fear of losing such a tasteless home. Maybe his own wasn't much better, he thought, not that it made any difference now.

'Are you feeling all right?' Her voice startled him. She was observing him from the doorway.

'I'm fine, I'm fine,' he assured her, pulling himself out of the armchair. He gave an unconvincing laugh. 'I was just miles away. That's all. I'd better go and get cleaned up, and have a shave.'

'Whatever you feel like. But remember you don't have to polish your shoes for this lot of guests.'

A vague suspicion that Susie was plotting to use the Simmondses for her own ends already lurked in the back of his mind. But he had no idea of what she could hope to achieve. There was no make-up today, he noticed. Immediately he felt tempted to get his own back after her remark the other night that he was always seeking approval. Instead he restricted himself to asking whether they were having ratatouille for lunch. She laughed. 'I thought you might come out with that one.' He shrugged and turned to pad upstairs, his dejection engulfing him again.

When he reappeared much later in corduroys and suede shoes, Susie regarded him carefully, but said nothing. She remembered him once saying, 'But I don't feel comfortable in jeans.' When she had teased in reply that perhaps in his case they might provoke an identity crisis, he had reacted angrily.

Susie kept silent waiting for him to volunteer some help. Just as she was about to suggest that he returned to the papers, he muttered that he would lay the table.

They both looked up on hearing the sound of tyres on gravel. 'And I was sure they were going to be hours late,' Susie remarked. 'Doesn't matter. Everything else's ready.' Voices and the slamming of car doors made them hurry. David resigned himself to the certainty of Susie welcoming them to Repro-Land.

Nancy waved to them as they appeared at the front door. 'We'll put the dog back in the car once he's had a run round.' Walt, the cocker puppy, was yapping in excitement as he ran in circles on the grass, egged on by the two children.

'No, bring him in too,' Susie insisted. 'We can all take him for a walk afterwards. Now that the mist's lifting it should be a beautiful afternoon.'

Nancy was amused at how David Rayner was taken aback by the friendly though off-hand way the twins greeted him. Obviously he was not used to boys and girls of seven who were so far from being shy. John came up from behind and smiled sheepishly to his hosts as if he had not met them before. The contrast between the father and the children was remarkable. They seemed to treat him like an elder brother who was a bit slow.

'What do you feed them on?' Susie asked as they ran out of the house again.

'She gives them intravenous injections of wholemeal vitamins,' John answered quickly. 'Even if fathered by me, no children of hers are going to have sand kicked in their faces.'

'Oh, you poor victim of rationing,' Nancy retorted. 'Listening to you, anyone'd think I wanted to turn back the tide of heredity and create a Californian super-race.'

'Right,' Susie said addressing the children. 'Let's get you sorted out first. What do you want to do? Run round the house, or outside? After lunch you can explore the wood. In fact you two can go and hide then we'll track you down with your dog.'

'With Walt?' the girl exclaimed disdainfully. 'But he's only a puppy. He's not fierce.'

'Well, I'm afraid the local hounds have Sunday off.'

John was highly amused when he heard they had not had time to lay the table. He regarded his map-reading as vindicated, and Nancy's scepticism confounded for once.

'Where's the cutlery?' he demanded. 'I must atone for my excessive efficiency.' David tried to persuade him to sit down and read the newspapers instead.

'No thanks. The pages of "background" material to camouflage the lack of progress are even worse than I feared.' He immediately checked himself, remembering how sensitive David Rayner was to suggestions that the Prime Minister had been abandoned. But once his host had left the room John turned from laying the table. 'And how are the locals down here facing up to Our Darkest Hour?' he asked Susie with a harsh edge to his voice. 'Gazing wistfully at their limited-edition prints of the Battle of Britain? Christ, the nationalistic clichés the press are handing out make me feel sick. It's just to make us feel noble about leaving the PM to his fate.' He looked back at his work. 'That doesn't look right. But then I always seem to get them the wrong way round.'

'Ask the Foreign Office protocol department,' Susie called back through the hatch, but immediately regretted her flippancy. Although grateful for John's attempt to help, she pulled him to one side when he came to ask for more knives. 'Do go and get David to give you a drink,' she urged him quietly. 'Otherwise he'll feel uncomfortable.'

Susie hated the formality of the dining-room, particularly the portrait of David's great-grandfather, but they were far too many to sit round the kitchen table. While spooning out the curry, she told them that if David had had more luck the day before it would have been pigeon pie. Then, when he offered John and Nancy some wine with a warning about its roughness, Susie joked about his salesmanship. 'Whenever he invited me to something,' she added to Nancy, 'he always tried to make it sound wildly unattractive.' David Rayner showed no reaction as he filled the twins' glasses with the Coca-Cola Susie had bought the day before.

Susie went on to tell John that David's family had been wine-shippers. 'When I first heard about it, I had frightful visions of him doing all that turkey-gobbling bit between the tonsils. But thank God, it didn't seem to interest him that much.'

'Oh?' John turned to him with a mock innocent expression. 'Didn't you need it for the Foreign Office entrance exam?'

'The country-house weekend test went out before my time,' Rayner answered with a tight smile, and then relapsed into his worries again. Susie asked John which college he had been to at Oxford.

'Balliol,' he answered.

'How funny. I had a friend who used to go out with a Balliol man. But then she did spend a lot of time at Oxford parties. The poor girl became known as "the flying buttress" because she always seemed to be propping up some drunk.'

Apart from a few curt replies, David Rayner did not speak during the meal. Nancy and John glanced in his direction a couple of times, wondering what the matter was, but Susie managed to maintain the momentum of conversation. A nervous energy drove her to make the occasion a success, if only to defy the atmosphere of the house.

After coffee in the sitting-room, David said that he felt too sleepy to venture out. So sending the twins on ahead to the wood, Susie organized gumboots for John and Nancy.

Outside, the sun was red and the sky a hazy grey like a Japanese painting. Although still mild, it felt as if there could be a frost that night. At first Nancy suspected there had been a tacit arrangement that David stayed behind. But once they were across the road and into the field, she sensed Susie's relief at being alone with the two of them. It came as no surprise when she began to walk with her head lowered swaying from side to side, and then jerked upright to ask how David seemed to them, as if it was a question which had just occurred to her. 'I know it must seem a bit odd that I should be so worried about him, after what you must think of us as a couple.'

John muttered that all relationships had their ups and downs. Susie regarded him sharply. Then she began to explain, rushing some bits and pausing to consider at other moments. She told them how David had been attracted by her disregard for convention, but had at the same time always wanted her to be the perfect future ambassadress. 'Rather like the way men seem to want the virgin and the whore all rolled into one.' Realizing her unintended pun, she smiled quickly. Then as they skirted the edge of the wood, she recounted the events in Paris including the episode with François, and David's arrival.

'Isn't life strange? It really couldn't have been much more of a disaster all round. And yet the way I managed to mess everything up brought us together. I really did love David for accepting it. Well, maybe he couldn't deep inside him, but at least he never blamed me then. The problems only started when he got this thing about moving out of London to be in the country again after his parents' house was sold. It was all a fixation with roots and the past, I suppose. He knew I didn't really want to, so he put our flat on the market and accepted an offer without discussing it properly. That was the start of our cold war, and only then did he begin bringing up what had happened in Paris. Presumably because he knew he was in the wrong, going about things that way.' Susie found herself watching Walt as he bounced in and out of the low bramble. She made a movement as if to shake herself out of a daydream. 'Aren't we neglecting the twins?'

'Yup,' Nancy sighed. 'I reckon we'd better get our tracking act together.'

When they had finally rounded up the children and returned to the house, Susie pressed them to stay for a high tea or an early supper. She joked about the unaccustomed excess of food while afraid of a sense of flatness after their departure; cleaning up in an emptied house.

Finally, with waves and repeated calls of thanks from the whole family, the old Renault estate car started to move out into the road. A BMW coming round the corner swerved to avoid them. John Simmonds braked hard and the engine stalled. Nancy looked back to make a face of humorous resignation.

'Well, David was certainly in a strange mood,' John said after a few minutes' driving. 'Christ, what an existence cut off down here.'

'But glad we came?' Nancy teased him with all the justifications he had made for accepting the invitation. She asked him what he was thinking. He first looked in the driving mirror and saw that the twins were already asleep. 'Oh, I was just wondering about Susie's lover and the phone call from the restaurant. Do you think she's right?'

'What about?'

'That it must have been François who rang the embassy.'

'It's not unknown for men to have a very strange sense of humour.' Nancy looked sideways at him. 'Some much more than others, thankfully.'

'I wonder what David's reaction was,' he said.

'We don't even know whether she told him. But even so, I hardly see David being able to imagine anyone behaving like that. I wouldn't have thought he really understands devious mentalities.'

18

The wind had risen again during the night. Trees had brought down telephone lines in the West Country according to the seven o'clock news. And along Rayner's route from the Underground gusts raised miniature cyclones of dead leaves and litter. The headache from the previous night's whisky became worse with the tension of his neck and temples in the cold.

Once again his mood fluctuated between resignation and lurches of fear low in the stomach. Every murmur in the corridor outside his office would sound like doctors discussing a terminal case in hushed tones. Every glance from a colleague would seem to recognize the angel of career-death hovering over him. He half-expected the guard on the front desk to examine his pass suspiciously. Then while waiting for the lift he imagined the man's eyes pointed at his back. Telling himself to get a grip, he prepared to greet any other early bird on the third floor in as calm a manner as he could muster.

To his surprise, Nigel Pannet was the first person he saw on stepping out of the lift. His assistant cursed as the coffee slopped over the lip of the plastic beaker, scalding his fingers.

'Bit out of character to be in this early, isn't it Nigel?' Rayner said, finding his act easier than he had feared. Pannet observed him for a moment. He seemed to have a truculent air, which Rayner put down to Monday-morning surliness. His eyes were puffy and the curly hair refused to stay down.

'Can we have a chat?'

'Certainly,' Rayner replied, guessing what it was about. He handed him the keys to his office. 'Go ahead and grab a pew while I get some of that disgusting stuff as well.' As the machine clicked and gushed in response to his coin, Rayner glanced up and down the corridors. The white walls, strip lighting and darkened offices down one side gave a claustrophobic effect. He was reminded of the passage to the car-park in Cologne-Bonn airport.

Pannet did not wait for him to sit down. 'Honestly chief, the way things are going at the moment makes me feel a right idiot. How can I hold the fort and repel inquisitive boarders when I haven't the foggiest notion of what's happening?' His self-righteous tone was almost amusing. Rayner gave a sympathetic grimace to signify that life was tough. He did not blame Pannet for feeling resentful, and yet what did the boy expect? Junior grades had no right to expect a full picture. But the most immediate reason for not letting his assistant in on his thoughts was quite simply a lack of trust. Pannet's loyalty was unashamedly to his own career.

'Listen, Nigel, I would certainly prefer to tell you all. It'd be a weight off my shoulders at least. But for your own good, it's better that you don't know. I may have things wrong, and run into a lot of flak as a result, so it's in your interest to be kept out of it.' Rayner felt rather pleased with his deceitfully heroic little excuse. 'But as you've probably guessed there are problems in Cologne, I strongly suggest that you keep any speculation to yourself.'

'So much for the "full and frank exchange between allied services",' Pannet muttered derisively and bent forward to flick a dozy fly from the edge of the desk.

'Well, you can't really blame the Germans. Until they've got it sorted out at their end, they're bound to be scared that the whole affair might blow up into an unnecessary scandal. You know how tricky things are in Bonn at the moment.'

'And does that mean the pressure's off us?'

'No, of course it doesn't.' Rayner was about to explain why they had to tread carefully, when he realized that the director-general would probably use exactly the same arguments.

At five to ten he took the lift to the sixth floor. Discreetly checking the knot of his tie, he went through to announce himself to Mrs Duckworth in the outer office. Her expression had led to one of Pannet's better nicknames – the offended llama. She was a pillar of the security establishment in every sense, Rayner thought. Her solid body was armoured in a navy-blue suit, she had a thick neck ringed by fake pearls, and wore bullet-proof glasses.

'If you'd care to take a seat, Mr Rayner. The director-general is still busy.' Her tone emphasized that it was the normal state of affairs on the sixth floor. He crossed to the pair of low armchairs, wondering whether the freeze was reflected from above or whether it was her usual manner.

The long wait with Mrs Duckworth avoiding his eyes made his thoughts twist back and forth between an understanding of the need for diplomatic hypocrisy and frustrated anger over the lack of progress in the hunt. When a buzzer eventually sounded on her intercom, she told him he could go through. Worse than the bloody dentist, Rayner thought.

'Take a seat,' the director-general told him brusquely as he finished looking through a report. To Rayner it sounded just short of an order to a disobedient gundog.

The only light in the long room came from the three windows down the side. Rayner was surprised that the director-general had not switched on his famous spot-lamps. Although ranking as a Permanent Under-Secretary entitled him to curtains and wallpaper along with a selection from the Department of the Environment's category three pictures, he had chosen plain walls, woven blinds and abstract canvases. It was for this reason that the office was sometimes referred to as the Hampstead penthouse.

As soon as the director-general put down the report, Rayner sensed that on this occasion there would be little informality. He raised his eyes to regard Rayner harshly. 'What in God's name has got into you? I just can't believe it.' He shook himself imperceptibly to act out a sense of stupefaction. 'First of all you deliberately miss a highly important group-head meeting. And as you know, I take the strongest exception to assistants being asked to lie on behalf of their superiors. Secondly, and *far* more seriously, you get some hare-brained fixation, then dash round Europe at public expense doing the *very* opposite to your task of fostering good relations with allied services.' Rayner began to explain but was silenced immediately.

'What? You mean you think it's in the national interest to tell the *Verfassungsschutz* that they're riddled with neo-Nazis?' Rayner opened his mouth to protest but the director-general rode him down. 'Because that's certainly the way it came across to them. You also seem to have forgotten that the function of the whole department is liaison. And liaison can only work when procedures are followed. Instead, you seem to have appointed yourself as some Mickey Mouse freelance, doing as you please without deigning to inform anybody else.'

To his dismay Rayner found that he could not muster a defence of his actions. He began to wonder if he was going crazy. Was Willi's distress a figment of his imagination? It remained the only support for his theory.

'As you know, we desperately need the West Germans,' the director-general continued 'With the run on the pound after the renewed rioting, we simply cannot afford to put their backs up.' His eyes searched Rayner's expression for a moment then he turned to gaze out of the window at the grey expanse. 'Anyway, even supposing Red Vanguard contained right-wing terrorists, what surely matters is that we nail them. As you must be aware, a destabilization strategy from either extreme is not much different when it comes down to it. Out of some crazy hope that it'll unleash "spontaneous resistance", the far Left wants to provoke us into "revealing our real dictatorial nature". While the extreme Right just tries to bring about authoritarian government.' The director-general made an impatient gesture at the need to reiterate the obvious.

Rayner was about to ask whether there was a lead on any other members of the group, but a survival instinct told him to remain silent. He showed no emotion as the director-general proceeded to warn him that although no official action would be taken at that stage, such behaviour undoubtedly prejudiced his career.

In the lift down from the sixth floor Rayner felt a weakness in his limbs. He had been left in no doubt that he had put up a monumental black against his record only three months before the annual confidential report. And perhaps the Allied Liaison Group was already the last of the backwaters; like town-twinning in the Foreign and Commonwealth Office. If this was America, the final stage would be as an unperson 'walking the halls', deprived of desk and office so as to force resignation. But a British bowler-hatting probably boiled down to the same thing, he reflected.

The only course left to save himself consisted of carrying on to prove he had been right. That meant contravening the edict which said the national interest required the three little monkeys act; seeing, speaking and hearing no evil. No, Rayner told himself with a new-found resolution. I didn't imagine Willi's reaction. He was upset in that stiff hurt way Germans have when their honour's at stake. But then asking himself what he would have done in Willi's position, Rayner wondered whether he had maligned him. Willi could have covered his own back, and yet still left him some freedom of manoeuvre. The director-general had made no reference to Bloch, so perhaps Willi had just warned his superiors about the right-wing infiltration theory, but fudged the details. How to keep a clean nose and a clean conscience at the same time.

Then Rayner forced himself to consider whether Sykes's caution against hasty theories might not have been right after all. A German connection almost certainly existed; the way the *Verfassungsschutz* had embarked on an internal inquiry under tight security was evidence enough. And yet his own assumption that Bloch had been involved in a German operation was no more than supposition.

Uncertain of where to start again, Rayner decided that it might be worth checking on the *Verfassungsschutz* denial that they had received Bloch's details. As the watch lists were dispatched simultaneously to allied services, Rayner decided to examine their own copy once again.

On reaching the first floor Rayner walked directly from the lift to the bank of filing cabinets in INTELLIG's conventional registry. There he bent to seek out the French watch list drawer.

'And did you track down your man?' Frances Campbell inquired drily behind him. Rayner's startled reaction made her laugh. 'I'm sorry I frightened you,' she said broadening her Scots accent.

'Er, no. It was really more of an exercise in checking watch list procedures,' he explained too hurriedly. Amused by his defensiveness, Frances Campbell felt he was almost too easy a target. 'The next allied liaison report will be dealing with the subject,' he added.

'Oh, really?' she replied, elongating the word. 'I look forward to reading it.' She gestured towards the filing system. 'Can I be of any help?'

'I'll manage, thanks very much.'

'You're welcome, Mr Rayner,' she answered with an enigmatic smile. Rayner cursed her under his breath. He was convinced that she got a kick out of putting men off their stride, especially if she judged them to be conceited. And the trouble with bloody INTELLIG, he told himself, is that they have to pretend they know everything.

Having found the French folder, he checked that the room was empty before laying it on the cabinet top. The usual photocopy of the preliminary signal was missing from the inside front cover. There was no sign of staple marks, so he guessed the folder had been changed. He rapidly flicked through the cards. As he now presumed, there was no longer any record of Raul Bloch.

He replaced the folder carefully in the file before running the drawer back in. Perhaps he had secretly suspected all along that the cover-up extended to the British end. With a dubious grunt, he decided that the main surprise was to find he was not surprised. Nor was he afraid. You damn well should be, you bloody idiot, he told himself.

On his way up in the lift he considered whether Frances Campbell might be involved, but decided that she would have acted differently if that were the case. For a moment he was tempted to question her, but then told himself it was not worth it. The card must have been removed over the weekend.

Christian Morgan remained the only person who could help him. It was hardly an encouraging thought. A man proud of rejecting all ideals. And yet a cynic like him might perhaps enjoy giving the cesspool a stir just for the hell of watching the reactions; those who panicked, those who slid away and those who pretended that there was no smell. *S'en foutisme* was probably the best policy, Rayner thought grimly. Christian was more than a mere survivor. He was one of those clever bastards who always managed to come out on top. No apparent effort. Just a look of amused surprise at their own success.

19

Rayner began by closing his eyes firmly. It was a vain attempt to shut out the loud conversation between three members of what Susie called the Repro-Land ratpack. Then half-raising his eyelids, Rayner observed the plump typist opposite pop a peppermint into her mouth before shifting back into the carriage seat with a historical romance. Ignorance is bliss, he thought harshly. He wondered if she ever bothered about anything outside her daily routine. She probably registered automatic horror at events like a planecrash or the kidnapping of the Prime Minister, but such realities were beyond her active concern. That was for the experts. She and her family and friends all paid their taxes for those sorts of things. Like a licence for the telly, which they could switch off if a programme made them feel uncomfortable.

Rayner's mood was not helped by the effort of controlling his impatience, which bordered on claustrophobia. Finally, at Reigate station, he only just managed to keep his temper during the jostle for the ticket barrier. Breathing a sigh of relief, he paused under the weak lights by the exit to the car park so as to select the right key in advance. But instead of driving off on his usual route home, he turned on to the main road which led to Gatwick airport. It started to rain. He switched on the wipers, slowing down a little until the dirt on the windscreen cleared. He had enough time.

Inside the terminal, Rayner went straight upstairs. Knowing that Special Branch had intensified its watch on air and seaports, he did not want to take any unnecessary chances in the departures hall. After selecting a seat in the corner of the bar, he made sporadic attempts to read his newspaper in between sips of whisky and listening to the announcements. Apparently one MP had described those campaigning against identity cards as 'terrorist fellow-travellers'. He put down the paper and went to check the arrivals board again. To his relief the Paris flight was shown to have landed. He then went to the lavatory before returning to the bar.

As he watched the entrance over the top of his folded newspaper, Rayner became increasingly afraid that Morgan might have decided at the last moment against coming. The piped music got on his nerves. Susie had once called it 'aural valium', but he always seemed to experience the opposite effect. Rayner had almost persuaded himself that Morgan would not appear when the Frenchman halted just inside the double doors. He wore a blazer and dark-grey trousers. A black briefcase and Burberry completed the impression of the typical *cadre supérieur*. Morgan spotted him and walked over. He slid into the armchair between the other side of the table and the wall. His signal to the waiter had evidently been perfected with years of practice. Rayner could not help thinking how Pannet would envy it.

'I see what you mean about the computerization of passport controls,' Morgan murmured in French, leaning sideways as he extracted a packet of Marlboro from his blazer pocket.

'Did you use an alternative passport?' Rayner asked, also avoiding English. Morgan nodded brusquely. He looked up to order a cognac before the waiter reached the table. The man acknowledged, swivelling back the way he had come all in one movement.

'So,' Morgan said. 'You're convinced that the Red Vanguard is really a front for the extreme Right.'

'Shall we say it seems a strong possibility. And it also appears to be a possibility which could embarrass certain people.'

'You mean too much has been said about terrorism being a left-wing disease.' Rayner inclined his head.

'Well,' Morgan sighed. 'I have done a little discreet research into the subject.' He paused, bending back in his chair to allow the waiter room. After the man had left, he lifted the glass in an ironic toast, then put it to his lips.

'But Christian,' Rayner said sitting forward with his forearms on the table. 'I first need as much background as possible. In Britain we haven't really had anything to do with this Black Orchestra business.' Rayner ran his hand back through his hair. The gesture made Morgan suddenly notice the strain in Rayner's face. Its boyish quality seemed to have vanished. Morgan felt a strange pity. 'Perhaps', Rayner added, 'our inexperience might be why they chose us as their target.'

Morgan answered with a twist of his mouth to show he was doubtful. 'Well, I'd better give you a quick beginner's course, then.' The Frenchman pulled back his sleeve to check how much time remained before his return flight. 'I will need to go back to the Sixties to outline the origins of the "Neo-Fascist International", as some now call it. But first of all we must be clear about the different character types which make up the extreme Right, both fascist and arch-traditionalist. These can best be categorized as "cowboys", "romantics" and "professionals". The cowboys are obviously the young toughs.'

'The streetfighters?'

'Yes. They're mainly used for attacking leftist newspapers, student demonstrations. That sort of thing. For the most part they're Hitler worshippers, even in Italy where they despise the Benito generation of old admirals and senators. The romantics are mainly aristos and right-wing intellectuals.'

'And how do you define the "professionals"?'

'They're the ones in the forces, police and secret services. In the French Army, legionnaires and paras. In Italy it's paras and carabinieri while of course the old SID military intelligence was run by them.'

'And the new organization after the purge?'

'No different really. The Christian Democrats want them as a last ditch in case the Cocos get too many votes next time round. Or if there's another scandal which really blows the top off the volcano.' Rayner's eyes flickered sideways as a man entered the bar looking around.

'While we're on the subject,' Morgan continued, 'I might as well cover Italy now; especially one of the key characters. Someone of whom I'm sure you've heard.' Rayner looked up expectantly. 'General Saletti, the former SID chief.'

'Saletti? But I met him once at a NATO conference in Brussels.'

'And were you aware that he had been involved in Prince Valerio Borghese's attempted *coup d'état* back in 1970? Operation Tora Tora. Funny choice of code-name considering they were bankrolled by the Americans.' Rayner looked mystified for a moment before remembering it was the Japanese battlecry for Pearl Harbor.

'The General kept in the background between 1969 and 1973 during the "Strategy of Tension". He's no fool, so he must have learnt some lessons from that mess. It certainly showed the need for special training. And above all that it was mad to use cowboys. Like that idiot who threw the grenade at the police memorial service and claimed he was a leftist. His story didn't stand up for more than a couple of hours.' Whatever Morgan's moral stance on the subject, he could not conceal his professional dismay at such blundering.

'Even the supposed professionals in the SID allowed their main effort to be uncovered later. You remember, David. December '69.' Morgan relaxed in his chair. 'Five bombs in a day including the Piazza Fontana massacre in Milan. Of course they weren't helped when their over-zealous comrades in the police chucked that anarchist out of a fourth-floor window. From then on the whole frame-up started to fall to pieces fast . . . well, fast for Italian justice. But their biggest disappointment was the coup attempt in December 1970.'

'You're certain General Saletti was involved?' Rayner asked.

'Yes. But not in the way you'd imagine.' Morgan gave a faint smile. 'Borghese's *coup de farce* was really a set-up without the old Black Prince realizing. The whole thing was in fact a two-step plan. Borghese and his fascist cowboys were encouraged to seize strategic points in Rome by their friends in military intelligence. But these "friends", Saletti included, did not let on that the real plot was for Army units to come charging in immediately afterwards pretending to save the nation from the fascists and the Cocos at the same time. The Army above politics, and all that *bullshit*.' Morgan relished the Americanism with another of his fleeting smiles.

'What went wrong then?'

'Several Army officers objected to the part of the SID plan which said that Borghese's lot had to be shot down for the sake of realism. So one of them tipped off Borghese just as the operation started. Not surprisingly, the old man and his thugs all did a quick about-turn, and a very fast fade into the night. Not a whisper to begin with. It resembled the Mafia's *omerta*. Then when a report of the aborted attempt slipped out, Andreotti was forced to instigate an official inquiry. The General . . . colonel he was then, managed to keep his name out of the inquest. His boss became a token sacrifice, otherwise it was typical whitewash.

'For present purposes, the main result was the way the General evidently swore that in future there'd be no more amateur dramatics leading to other fiascos. Infiltration of the reds had to be done effectively, or not at all. No more of that turning up at a couple of demonstrations, yelling a few slogans and reckoning you looked a full-blooded leftist. There had to be a total cut-out. Not just "plausible deniability" in the short term.' Morgan paused, raising his head to listen for a moment to an announcement, then resumed.

He went on to trace the origins of the French side of the network and how members of the OAS, in particular Jean Calvet, developed their contacts. 'Starting along the Mediterranean then. In the old days Portugal was quite a centre. Calvet's clearing-house in Lisbon was protected by the Portuguese secret police until the revolution changed everything. A detachment of marines discovered all the files intact because the "correspondents" made a run for it. That was a purely French operation, OAS and the Catholic City lot in the Army.'

'And now?' Rayner asked.

'Things might be starting there again, but nothing to get excited about for the moment. There've been one or two informal talks with some Army officers, that's all. Now, Spain's very different. It's always been vital to the French and the Italians. Number one bolthole as well as permanent residence with police protection in Madrid, arms shipments via Barcelona and conferences in Andorra. Not surprising of course. It's where the Right's been in power the longest, and even since Franco's machines were switched off back in '75, it's still the safest refuge. The Army, *Seguridad* and civil guard will be able to go on making sure of that, no matter how many coup attempts they mess up.'

'But is there much active co-operation with the General and Calvet's lot?' Rayner asked. Morgan shook his head. 'The Spanish Right's the most xenophobic of all.'

'Not always,' Rayner corrected. 'Some years back the IRA had some help from a group of ultra-rightists in the Spanish Army wanting to help a Catholic crusade. And that was at the same time as the Basque ETA guerrillas were helping them too.'

Morgan lifted his hand in acknowledgment. 'And did you know how the Basque Nationalist Party got most of their weapons?' Rayner shook his head. 'Well, in Paris during May '68 when it looked like civil war, the Gaullist youth were given a convoy full of automatic weapons. But after the crisis was over, they fell out with their parent party, and refused to hand them back. Then when they realized they had no option, they told the Basques to help themselves one night. It was quite a haul.' Morgan signalled to the waiter once again.

'Right. Let's just quickly finish off the Mediterranean. Things are getting going again in Greece in a big way. The purge of the military police might never have happened. As you probably know there's a strong link with Italy since the days when the Greek Colonels helped the Italian Right during the strategy of tension. There's still the old idea of a league of Mediterranean military dictatorships.' Morgan stared down at the condensation on his glass. 'I have also heard a whisper that the Americans will channel help via Italy to begin with. If that's the case, then it means the General's definitely back in favour on *both* banks of the Potomac.' He looked up with a sardonic expression. Rayner grimaced in reply.

'Anyway,' Morgan shrugged, 'now the main axis. The Paris-Rome Axis,' he added with mirthless humour. 'The connection is nothing new. You might perhaps have heard of the Paris bomb explosions during the Spanish Civil War in September 1937. The idea was to make the French Army restless and frighten the Popular Front off helping their brother reds in Spain. And for that little operation, Emanuele, the head of Mussolini's service, used an officer in French military intelligence to do his recruiting.'

'As a cut-out?'

'That was the intention, but then the clowns went and used Italian gear.'

'Presumably the General and Calvet pay more attention to that sort of thing.'

'Yes. They use intermediaries to do the shopping. For a psy-op they would never take anything from their stocks of material filched from the Army. It must be sterile. Non-traceable. That's why arms like the Czech Skorpion are so popular. The serial numbers aren't stamped deep, so there is less problem removing them. And also there's no risk of such material being traced back from end-user certificates.

'Well, the present French-Italian link came in the late Sixties. It's even said that Calvet helped plan the Milanese bomb blast in December '69. Certainly officers borrowed some of their French counterparts' ideas on countering Coco subversion by indoctrinating their conscripts with Nationalist-Catholic propaganda. It never worked of course, in fact it probably helped the Cocos if anything. But the most important bit was the way the alliance was organized. With France out of NATO, close liaison between ordinary French and Italian serving officers was too conspicuous.'

'So the Italian secret service and your Swimming Pool . . .'

'Exactly. They were told by their respective governments to keep close links in order to fight red terrorists. So it all had a nice official blessing. The General kept his record clean as far as the outside world was concerned, and Calvet had his allies at all levels in the Swimming Pool.'

Morgan paused to take a drink. Rayner watched him reflectively. 'Tell me, Christian,' he said. 'Why do you hate the Swimming Pool so much?'

'*Bof*,' Morgan replied. 'Hate, no. Dislike, yes. I think there are several reasons. One I've already told you. They're a stupid arrogant lot. A real closed shop of *retro* aristos. But more importantly, people like me feel very uncomfortable with such "idealists" playing around. Ordinary politicians are much more predictable and easy. The Swimming Pool goes over the top at times . . .' Morgan gave a faint grin to apologize for the unintended joke. 'Risk of flooding. You see, they're not always very clever over who they associate with.'

Rayner suddenly found himself wondering if Morgan was an inheritor of the Talleyrand tradition. Perhaps he'd work for a Communist regime just as effectively. 'So basically, Christian, you don't like the way the Swimming Pool risks sinking the boat, instead of just giving it a healthy rock.'

'I never said that,' Morgan replied looking back evenly at Rayner. 'But I think it would be correct to say that most of the French security world believes that it's correct to *plan* a pre-emptive move in case the Cocos ever get the whip hand. Remember what I said about the Christian Democrats in Italy not wanting a purge of their security services. But at the same time I, and many of my colleagues, don't feel at all comfortable when there are characters in the Swimming Pool like de Castezac, who've always pushed for *active* counter-revolution.'

'Tell me a bit about him.'

'Oh. He used to be one of the great believers in that religious and patriotic indoctrination programme. Until even he had to accept that it wasn't working.'

'So now he opts for "propaganda of the deed". Only turned inside out.' There was a distinct silence.

'*Ouai*,' Morgan agreed eventually.

'And this de Castezac character,' Rayner asked, controlling his voice. 'Might he also have been Raul Bloch's case officer when he did a few dirty tricks against synagogues or the Left?'

Avoiding Rayner's eyes, Morgan shrugged, then examined his watch.

20

With his mind in a turmoil of speculation after Morgan's guarded tip, Rayner arrived home to find Susie reading. It seemed to have become her favourite pastime, he noted distantly while passing through the sitting-room. 'You'll go blind there,' he warned with a nod towards the table lamp. Susie did not move at first. 'Thank you for your concern, kind sir,' she murmured before looking up to watch the study door close. She shook her head slightly with eyebrows raised, then returned to her book.

Susie soon found that her concentration had been upset. Oh Jesus, she muttered to herself. Why can't he say something?

After shutting the door of his study, Rayner dropped into the armchair, but a short while later stood up to move around the room. For the first time in years he had a sharp desire for a cigarette, but he couldn't ask Susie for one. Rayner had hoped that Morgan's information would clarify things and therefore reassure him, but he now knew what a ridiculously optimistic attitude that had been. Of course he had been aware of neo-fascist terror groups and their proliferation over the last few years, but now he knew how difficult it was to say where the crazies stopped and the professionals began.

He remembered General Saletti from their brief introduction as an impressive and charming man. Not very tall, but distinguished with silver hair. The Americans had backed his appointment to JAID, the Joint Allied Intelligence Directorate outside Brussels. Morgan's reference to the increased favour shown him by Washington was very disturbing. The Americans were not exactly renowned for a discriminating choice when it came to protégés. The trouble was they were also less than subtle when it came to concealing their motives. In fact their denials had been so implausible in the past that they made themselves scapegoats for almost any disaster abroad. Rayner was tempted to believe that de Castezac was not part of some Company game-plan; if only because the Prime Minister could not have been seen as a threat to western defence by even the most paranoid of CIA strategists.

Rayner was startled by a rap on the door as it opened. He looked round the back of his armchair spilling some of his drink. Susie laughed. 'If you're going to be so jumpy, perhaps we'd better install an illuminated "No Entry" sign for you to switch on.' She glanced round. The atmosphere of his study depressed her more than anything else in the house. She noticed the old copies of *Country Life* and the *Field* on the floor by the table. No one else entered the room, she thought, so who was he trying to convince, apart from himself?

Susie stopped her train of thought, then exhaled. 'Right,' she said, forcing a bright tone. 'Why don't you go and open some wine while domesticated little Susie dishes up?'

Rayner had been about to say that he would make a sandwich later, but now he could not refuse. He ran a hand over the lower half of his face before summoning the energy to haul himself to his feet.

After a meal during which Rayner had given only brusque replies to her attempts at conversation, he pushed back his chair, then reached for his plate to take it over to the sink. He stopped, unable to ignore Susie's stare.

'I know you're in a hurry to get back to your privacy,' she said with quiet firmness. 'I also know that you've got a lot on your mind. But haven't you anything to tell me?'

'I'm sorry my small talk wasn't up to scratch.'

'I didn't mean that,' she said, controlling her anger. She took a deep breath. 'Something is bugging you badly. I know of course that you've got to be security-conscious, and all that. But wouldn't it help if you talked about it a bit? I've never been indiscreet about anything that mattered.'

'Never been indiscreet? I can think of one thing everyone else seemed to know about pretty fast.' Rayner regretted his retort the moment his words came out. It seemed as if some inner mechanism beyond his control had triggered them off.

Susie regarded him with a mixture of scorn and despair. She shook her head in disbelief. 'You'd better go back to your little pipedream land. Go and stare at that ghastly old photo of me looking wistful. It was never me, all that English rose number. But you'll still go on telling yourself I changed.' Susie stopped, then uttered a short bitter laugh. 'How stupid of me. I've only just twigged. That photo's like your other memories. They're all of perfect moments in time which never existed.' Susie pushed aside her plate before lighting a cigarette. She exhaled to the side as she examined him closely. 'Poor David. You'd better go back to your secret little world, Knight of the Sad Countenance.'

Rayner had no idea what to say in reply. He could not persuade her that it was pointless to argue over a silly remark which had slipped out. So, deciding it would be better to smooth things over when she had calmed down, he gave an apologetic shrug as he turned to leave the room.

21

The next morning Rayner went straight down to INTELLIG. But all he could discover from traditional files and the computer was that de Castezac had transferred to the Swimming Pool from the French Army active list five years before. Rayner again debated the risks of taking Frances Campbell into his confidence. She was the best person to try American sources on one of her frequent journeys to Grosvenor Square where the CIA London Station's terminal was lined straight into the main computer at Langley, Virginia.

The problem was that a name like de Castezac could not be camouflaged with spelling variations. And it would certainly stick out from the routine pile of watch list clarification requests. The greatest danger would come if de Castezac figured in any Company game-plan along with the General. In such an event there would be an automatic hold and flashing lights to alert against the inquiry originator. Rayner told himself it made better sense to try other sources first.

At any rate he was now, at last, pointing in the right direction, thanks to Morgan fingering de Castezac. Rayner reflected ruefully on the way he had become obsessed with the computer sabotage and set off on his German wild-goose chase. But events in Cologne were still not clear. Either de Castezac's helper in the *Verfassungsschutz* had simply decided that wholesale sabotage was less risky than the elimination of a few key entries. Or it was a blind as well. Certainly the deliberate recruitment of German speakers supported the diversion theory.

Exhilarated by a general sense of progress, Rayner returned to his office, running up the stairs. He closed the door behind him before ringing his opposite number on the Defence Intelligence Staff. Implying that a colleague wished to approach de Castezac, Rayner requested everything obtainable for background briefing.

'Rings a bell, that name,' the gunner major replied. 'Wasn't he 1st Hussars? That's the Frogs' armoured-car para regiment based at Pau in the Pyrenees.'

Rayner bridled at the forced pompous tone. It seemed the last defence of the irredeemably middle-class officer who had been passed-over. There was not the slightest trace of self-parody in his manner. 'That's quite possible,' Rayner replied.

'Bit of time ago, though.'

'Quite. Since then he must have been on the intelligence side before transferring to the Swimming Pool. But tell me. Would he have had much to do with the Foreign Legion?'

'Their para battalions, yes, that's possible. And the Legion armoured-car regiment almost certainly. As for the other units, it would have depended on the operations or exercises which the *Force d'Intervention* carried out then.' The monstrous attempt at an accent made Rayner shudder at the thought of how French officers reacted to the major. Assured that he would have the details by the end of the day, Rayner thanked him for his help. He did not notice how his own voice had instinctively taken on an arrogant drawl.

Rayner had been tempted to ask for a photograph of de Castezac if available, but that would have risked too much for a personal whim. Now that the hitherto abstract conspiracy had begun to take on an identifiable form, he longed to know how the French officer looked. The baddies in black *képis*, he smiled grimly. Or rather, a deeper shade of grey. The Legion's motto was *Legio Patria Nostra Est*. Perhaps the Swimming Pool had something similar. *L'état c'est nous*, for example?

Rayner saw to his surprise that it was still only half-past nine. He braced himself for the next telephone call, wondering how reliable the old pals' act remained.

In the taxi Rayner leant back into the corner of the seat. It was comforting to huddle in his old midnight-blue overcoat with the velvet collar. He remembered showing it to Susie for the first time with coy pride. But her curious reaction implied that the style was the preserve of senior diplomats, making it sound almost like wearing a club tie before election as a member.

He was reminded of his resolution to buy her a present to make up for his stupid remark. There should be time to stop in Knightsbridge on the way back. That had been in the back of his mind when suggesting a rendezvous outside the Serpentine restaurant. The transparency of his request for what Security termed an 'ambulatory meeting' had embarrassed him. But to his surprise Ronnie Deakin's acceptance had not contained an ironic undertone.

The traffic was almost solid. Rayner extracted his fist from the depths of the coat pocket to check the time. He made a face even though a reasonable margin remained, then looked out of the window beside him. The man in the next car who held the top of the steering-wheel with both hands twisted his wrist to do the same. It's as infectious as yawning, Rayner thought distantly as he considered Deakin's likely attitude.

Although not his closest colleague during the years with the Friends, Rayner had known him better than most. Ronnie and his wife had once come to supper in Royal Crescent days. It would have been more often if Susie had not taken an aversion to him. Rayner had to admit she was often a perceptive judge of character, although of course sweeping in her comments. *Are they all like him?* she had inquired after the Deakins left. But when he asked what that was supposed to mean, she tried to drop the subject. Feeling forced to justify his association, he had exaggerated Deakin's interest and importance. Rayner shied away from a stronger description of the relationship, mainly because Deakin tended to claim almost anyone mentioned in conversation as a friend.

Once in the Park, Rayner told the driver to stop at the end of the bridge over the Serpentine. An American couple complaining cheerfully of the cold seized upon the taxi while he paid the fare. The wind gusted across the expanse of water below causing surface ripples. Rayner turned away to look for Deakin. There was no sign of him outside the concrete arches and glass of the restaurant complex. For a moment his eye was caught by a child stiffly bundled in woollens shuffling ankle-deep through a drift of leaves.

Just as Rayner was about to see if Deakin had been waiting for him inside, a car drew up. The passenger-door was opened from the inside.

'Too cold out for you?' Rayner asked once he had settled himself in the passenger-seat. Deakin gave him a mysterious knowing look. 'Not exactly, old man,' he said in his rasping voice. 'Though I suppose it depends on what you mean by cold.'

While Rayner stared at him inquisitively Deakin kept glancing in the rear-view mirror without moving his head. 'Shall we drive a little to check? Or do you already accept that you're as worthy of study as London's back-doubles?'

'What the hell are you on about, Ronnie?'

'Then we'd better check,' Deakin replied. He pulled out from the kerb, accelerating towards the Alexandra Gate. In a deliberately matter-of-fact tone Deakin asked if he had come in a black-cab via Marble Arch, then rattled off a licence number. Rayner agreed that he had, though adding that he did not usually look at the registration plate before climbing into a taxi.

'Well, obviously you never noticed your tail.'

'In a car?' Rayner asked trying not to allow the feeling of shock to become apparent.

'No, a scooter thing. Clipboard and blue crash-helmet. Playing at trainee cabbie doing "the Knowledge". An old favourite. Luckily your choice of Hyde Park made him conspicuous.' Lost for a reply, Rayner gave a defensive and meaningless shrug. Deakin's man-of-the-world act would gall him under any other circumstance, but now he felt vulnerably amateur.

They just beat the lights at the Alexandra Gate, Deakin swinging the car left without having indicated. Then he drove flat out alongside the park towards Apsley House. In Park Lane Deakin slalomed through the traffic to the left, then swerved down the ramp of the underground car park.

'Not so scenic, but a little more intimate,' Deakin remarked, suppressing his satisfaction. He switched off the engine. They sat in silence looking out into the half-darkness. The heater had made the car stifling so Deakin wound down his window. There was a hollow resonance of dripping water and the dull hum of a generator in the distance.

'Seems it's about time you were sent on a Personal Security refresher, David,' he remarked cheerfully. 'Or are the cares of state making you blind to your surroundings?'

'I was never a jungly.'

'You don't have to tell me that, old man. So what's a nice canapé-pusher like you doing with a shadow? Been a naughty boy . . . or too clever by half?' Deakin continued to eye him. 'Home-team interest, or the opposition?'

'Opposition?' Rayner said with a harsh laugh. 'Blueland good. Redland bad.' He shook himself imperceptibly. 'Sorry, Ronnie. It's just that the spectrum of colours seems to be a mite distorted at the moment. Either that or I need my eyes tested.'

'Tell all to your old uncle. Always said I should have ghosted a problem page.'

Rayner could not help wincing at the forced jollity. Twisted in the seat with his left shoulder-blade against the door, he lifted his head to stare at Deakin diagonally. He suddenly realized how little he knew the man, despite their long stint together on the Western Europe desk. Deakin was four years older although the lined forehead and bags under his watery eyes made it look more. He had cured his drink problem just in time, but still retained the livid complexion of the English soak.

In contrast to his apparent Britishness, Deakin had always been an unrepentant Atlantic man. On his desk he used to keep a grip-and-grin photograph of himself and the Deputy Director of Central Intelligence in a leather frame. Next to it there had been an ashtray with the CIA seal. Rayner once wondered whether he also had matching cufflinks to be worn in the privacy of his own home. It was the sort of thing Americans and their satellites loved.

'Do you know a Swimming Pool officer called de Castezac?' Rayner asked.

'Come across him.'

'In a friendly fashion?'

'It wasn't pistols at dawn in the Bois de Boulogne.' Deakin gave another of the conspiratorial smiles he adopted when trying to mystify.

'What's he like?'

'Physically? Oh . . . dark hair, thin face. Looks like the humourless little French baron that he is. Slim . . . wiry. What they would have called light cavalry build. In fact de C. did the old course at Saumur, as far as I remember. Though I don't imagine he would have appreciated the initiation test if it was still going in his day. He's a real little prude. I'm not sure if Catholic puritans aren't worse than the Protestant variety.'

'Why, what was the test?'

'The Trinity, they called it. Thirty kilometres on horseback with three whores and three bottles of champagne along the way, all in three hours.' Deakin's grin allowed interpretation as either respect for the stamina required, or amusement at such an anachronism. Rayner ignored it.

'But the main point is that he's a real ultra.'

'Tridentine mass in combat kit?' Deakin quipped. 'Anyway, "Ultra" tends to be rather a relative term when dealing with that lot, as you know. The Swimming Pool is hardly the Quai d'Orsay after dark.'

'Precisely. And that means they're not content with "the extension of policy by underhand means", as one of our masters defined it. They make their own.' Deakin raised his eyebrows slightly, but did not voice any objection. He rummaged in his pockets, then stretched across Rayner's knees, having sighted his cigarettes on the shelf under the facia. A rich bout of coughing followed. Deakin had quit the bottle only because his job was on the line. But a cancer hospital did not present him with such an immediate or imaginable a threat.

'From what I can make of de Castezac,' Rayner persisted, 'he loathes politicians of all sorts, and presumably regards any who were associated with the Fourth Republic as out and out traitors.'

'But my dear David, as you must surely know, that is hardly a rare attitude for an officer trained in the shadow of Diem Bien Phu and Algeria. And as for your dark reference to Fourth Republic politicians, I've not heard anything to indicate they're actively planning a nasty against the President.'

'No, but that I think is because they've been warned off playing with firecrackers in their own backyard by the other French services.'

'So your implication is that de Castezac and his friends are ratfucking on the outside. I suppose you mean trying to give a general impression of governmental collapse in Europe.'

'It's not new.'

'It is in northern Europe, old lad, unless people haven't been telling me things. Well anyway, let's stop pussyfooting around. Your hypothesis is obviously that it was de Castezac's lot playing Red Vanguard. But where do the Krauts fit in?'

'Foreign Legion. One of them at least.'

Deakin looked impressed. 'Seems as if you've been doing some ferreting in your tea-breaks.' He then switched to a secret smirk. 'Unless, of course, a jealous little frog has been croaking.'

Rayner found it hard to restrain his anger. Fortunately Deakin had to wipe his eyes with the back of his wrist. He threw the cigarette out on to the greasy concrete before winding the window up again. With a hand on the steering-wheel, his middle finger began to play with the indicator lever.

'I'd already heard a whisper about your neo-Nazi conspiracy theory. Made me wonder if you were going off the tracks.'

'So what do you think now you've heard the revised version?'

Deakin turned his head to stare at him. 'The same,' he replied levelly. 'David, what in hell are you trying to do? You haven't gone rogue, yet you seem set on a kamikaze mission which'll blow allied liaison in Europe back to the stone age. We've never needed each other so much as now. You know the Yanks require constant reassurance that they can count on a united Europe.' Deakin sat staring at the horn for a moment, shaking his head to emphasize his incomprehension. 'And if it all turns out all right, what can be gained by setting off a fire-storm in Westminster? The politicians would go bananas. It's one thing for them to rap a few civil service knuckles to keep the crowd quiet. But in *this* case they'd panic for their own sakes, and that'd spell chaos.'

Rayner looked away from the earnest gaze which had accompanied the last part of his entreaty. He made a slight movement with his hands to indicate doubt. Deakin seized on this sign that he was not irrevocably committed to his course. 'Listen David,' he urged. 'I won't report this conversation, though God knows, I should. But please, promise me as an old friend, you'll chuck it in. You're getting yourself and your friends into a no-win situation fast.'

22

After returning from Knightsbridge, Rayner went to his office to assemble the necessary papers for the meeting of the crisis committee. Standing over his desk, he glanced up when his assistant entered. 'Hello, Nigel. How are things?' Without waiting for a reply he went on searching for his copy of the latest liaison status report.

'Perhaps you can tell me, chief.'

Struck by his tone, Rayner looked at Pannet sharply. 'What do you mean by that?'

'Haven't seen much of you, to put it mildly.'

'Listen, I know I haven't kept you abreast of developments. I'm sorry. But we'll have a session as soon as this meeting's over.'

'It might be an interesting one.'

'What, you mean the row over the cordon and search plan?'

'That, but also Sykes's merry men in SESLIG appear to be twitching with suppressed excitement. Something's in the wind.' Pannet looked at his watch. 'Hadn't you better be getting up there?'

The meeting in the conference room seemed little different from previous ones, except that those present were even more on edge. The director-general, who opposed the cordon and search plan, found that he had to brave the Home Secretary dangerously. His only consolation was to know that he had the full support of his group heads. The other ally was Bailey of the Anti-Terrorist Squad, but, since the Commissioner and the Home Secretary refrained from calling on him, he could only express his disagreement with looks and impatient shifts in his chair. News of a major row within Scotland Yard had reached the Department. According to the rumour Bailey's replacement was imminent.

The Commissioner had just started to outline the proposed cordon and search operation when Sykes's number two in SESLIG slipped into the room. He gave an apologetic look to the director-general, who had turned round to glare. Coming up behind Sykes, he bent to whisper in his ear. Eyes shifted in their direction from all round the table. An interruption had to be important. Rayner watched with fascination but, as usual, Sykes betrayed no emotion. He made a quick gesture to the director-general to excuse himself before rising to follow his subordinate.

During Sykes's absence Rayner found it difficult to concentrate on the Commissioner's proposed plan. The flat voice hardly commanded attention at the best of times.

When Sykes re-entered the room a little more than five minutes later, he walked straight to his place ignoring the stares. The Commissioner broke off, having lost the thread of his sentence.

'I'm sorry to interrupt, sir,' Sykes said standing by his chair. 'But I think the whole situation may well have changed.'

'What do you mean by that?' the Home Secretary demanded.

'It looks as if we may have located the terrorists.'

'Well, for God's sake go on man. Where the hell are they? Is the PM all right?'

'All I have been given so far is an address.'

'And we've been given upwards of four hundred,' Bailey burst out from the far side of the table. 'So what's so bloody special about yours?'

'It sounds as if Commander Sykes has a terrorist super-grass,' the director-general suggested with a satisfied expression. Sykes ignored this interruption. He fixed his gaze on his challenger. 'When it comes to intelligence, quantity is seldom a useful objective.'

'This is no time for petty jealousies,' the Home Secretary snapped. 'All I'm interested in is whether the information's correct.'

'Obviously, I can't be a hundred per cent certain, Secretary of State,' Sykes replied. He looked levelly at his questioner. 'But I'm prepared to put my career on the line if that'll save delay.' There was a moment of silence.

'Then why don't . . .'

'I thought it worth the risk of issuing a preliminary warning order to the SAS at Hereford before coming back. The helicopters are being stood to, ready for the close-quarter combat teams.'

'Well, there's not too much to lose if you're wrong. And assuming you're right, then we'd better get moving.' The Home Secretary looked around, not expecting disagreement. He turned to the director-general. 'Get your ops room to send FLASH HARRY. Start with the SAS of course, but otherwise only contact A Priority list for the moment.' The director-general's aide was already on his way to the door, but came to a halt as more instructions followed. 'And unless there is no countermanding order . . .' the Home Secretary added, flicking up his wrist to check the time, 'COBRA will assume overall control of operations as from twelve forty-five hours.' The aide left the room running. 'Any comments, Commander Sykes?'

'Yes, Secretary of State. We have two considerations to evaluate. Surprise and preparation. They are not entirely incompatible.'

'What do you mean?'

'Well, surprise is vital, but the SAS have obviously got to know the layout of the house, and in which room the terrorists are holding the PM. What I mean is that we don't want a drawn-out Barricade and Hostage situation if it can be avoided.'

'I take your point. How long do you think we'll need?'

'We cannot *risk* any more than two hours from the time the first observation team arrives. I would have thought that the best programme . . .'

The Home Secretary stopped him at this point and turned to the Commissioner. 'Sir Neil, would you have any objection to Commander Sykes running the show, under your direct control, of course?'

'Oh, none whatsoever, Secretary of State. He's our most experienced anti-terrorist planner.'

The adjutant of the SAS was looking out of the window at the two Puma helicopters on the square when the telephone rang. It was the preliminary warning order. After replacing the receiver he could not decide whether it was best to activate the full alert immediately in order to gain time. He reached for the intercom button.

'Colonel, it's Alistair. We've had a warning order from the Department.'

'What? FLASH HARRY?'

'No, not yet. They aren't absolutely sure it's the right location, but one of their senior men is prepared to lay his balls on the chopping block.'

'Well, by God I'll take the first swing at them if he messes up our boys' performance with a false alarm.' There was a long pause. 'Yes, press the tit now.' The adjutant twisted in his chair to reach the wooden box on the wall. From where he sat he could hear buzzers sounding down the corridor.

The commanding officer walked rapidly into his office. 'Right then. Where are Jamie and his boys?'

'They should be on their way back from Pontrilas,' the adjutant replied. The colonel had a momentary stab of fear that there would be a road crash. It was always the mundane accidents that took you unawares. 'Are they on net?'

'Damn well should be. I'll check to see that the signals troop has made contact.'

'Tell them to take it carefully.' They both turned to glance out of the window as the helicopters started their engines.

Wearing combat kit, but bareheaded because of the rotor draught, the squadron sergeant-major began to supervise the loading of the equipment into the helicopters. Everything was prepared in double quantity, while a reserve set remained ready at the Duke of York's barracks in London. The QMSI small-arms instructor stood waiting in civilian clothes having seen his set of cases on board. The armourer accompanying him held on to the suitcase which contained the specially checked Heckler & Koch magazines. Each team member would then load his own on arrival. The men around the helicopters came up to attention as the colonel approached wearing the suit he kept ready in his office. It was cold out on the windswept square. He held his arms close to his sides.

'Haven't forgotten the ammo have you Q?' the commanding officer shouted over the noise of the engines.

'Not this time, sir,' he grinned back.

'And what's the current dud ratio?'

'Two rounds out of twenty-three thousand.'

'I suppose you're going to tell me that the third's due soon according to the law of averages.'

'I'm not too worried on that score, sir.'

'It's good to hear that someone round here's keeping calm.' The colonel dropped his jocular manner. He slapped a fist against an open hand in front of his chest. 'It'd better not be a false alarm.' The others present nodded in silent agreement. 'Oh, where the hell are they?' he demanded. He glanced at his watch but did not see the time.

The colonel could not even remember how many minutes ago FLASH HARRY had been confirmed. He stood kicking his heels in impatience. The QMSI pointed in the direction of the main gate. A convoy of long-wheel-base Land Rovers in camouflage marking with headlights dipped swung round the tarmac in a wide curve. They halted in line some thirty metres from the two helicopters. Sixteen black figures climbed out, and the Land Rovers drove off towards the vehicle park.

'Right,' the colonel shouted to them. 'Before we get aboard, I just wanted to warn you that contact is not yet absolutely sure. But if their claim *is* correct, then it looks as if we stand a chance of achieving complete surprise. We'll be kept abreast of developments by radio during the flight. On arrival you'll be taken direct to a house of the same size and layout as the one in which they reckon the PM is being held. This'll give you the opportunity for a final rehearsal. Jamie, you come with me in the front one.'

The thudding roar increased as the two Pumas lifted off the ground. Their passengers had scarcely been given time to settle in the web canvas seats. The RAF flight sergeant heaved the rectangular door across to cut out the rushing wind. Once clear of the camp roofs the helicopters dipped their heads to accelerate away. The colonel signalled to Jamie Maclaren that he was going to join the pilot for a moment.

Maclaren put on the intercom headset. The engine and rotor noise were reduced to a background vibration. Once again he found that the sound of radio mush in headphones produced a relaxing, almost hypnotic effect. The clipped voices were given a detached authority. Orders screamed emotionally over the sound of battle were virtually a relic of the past. He knew that the approaching operation would have gone seriously wrong if the need for more than a few words arose. As they had always been told in training, professionalism was not needing to think twice.

Maclaren looked at the set faces opposite. He guessed that the identity of the hostage was scarcely in their thoughts. They usually despised the politicians who were so impressed by their human secret weapon. At such a time the Regiment joked about 'the big-match temperament' and the action replays on television. 'Who cares who wins', the parody of their motto, was another flippant way of distancing themselves from motive or policy. The execution of the operation for its own sake was what counted.

23

With the Commissioner seated alongside, Sykes took over the controller's position in the operations room. According to the digital clock blinking noiselessly in front of him, there were twelve minutes before the video unit on the left of the master console would be switched through to the Cabinet Office. The screen on the right would remain blank until the Zulu Control vehicle could be moved into position.

On the planning table just below them, the mock-up artists were putting the last touches to a layout of Lime Avenue. Sykes adjusted the swivel armchair, then put on his headset. The semi-darkened room, the spotlit table, the small flashing lights on the consoles and the impersonal voices in the earphones combined to give him a strangely disembodied sensation.

'First observation team turning into Lime Avenue from western T junction now.' Sykes acknowledged with a movement of his head, unsure whether the link controller could see. The two men from the Yard's C7 technical section were dressed as engineers in a Gas Board van. 'They have now halted just short of number twenty-two. No sign of activity outside number twenty-four. Awaiting instructions.' The operations officer dialled a number and passed Sykes the receiver. He glanced down at the pad in front of him. The London Electricity Board computer recorded the occupiers of number twenty-two as Mr and Mrs W. Hardcastle.

'Mrs Hardcastle?' Sykes inquired when a woman's voice answered. 'My name is Sykes and I am a police officer. We very much need your assistance on a vital matter. Would you be prepared to help us?' She sounded flustered and uncertain. 'Tell her if necessary,' the Commissioner mouthed to him.

'Mrs Hardcastle, if you do what I and other police officers advise, you will be absolutely safe. Now, could you tell me if you have any children in the house?'

'No. No, they're all at school, aren't they?'

'Good. Now just outside your house there is a Gas Board van with two men inside, who are in fact plain-clothes police officers. They will come to your door in a few moments, carrying some equipment. Will you please let them in, and they will explain everything you need to know. Now if you want to check my identity or that of the officers, all you have to do is ring Scotland Yard direct.' Sykes flicked his fingers. His assistant poised, ready to tap out the number of the Scotland Yard switchboard controller. 'But I would be very grateful if you could help us straight away because somebody's life is in danger.'

'What's this all about then? It's not . . .'

Sykes signalled to the observation team's link controller. 'Mrs Hardcastle, all I can say for the moment is that some men we want to interview may be in the next-door house. Now, please go and open your door. There's nothing to worry about, I assure you.' Sykes heard the sound of the doorbell. He sensed her indecision. 'Go on, Mrs Hardcastle. I'm sure we can depend upon you.' With relief he heard her put the receiver down on the table. A few moments later he heard low voices in the background, then someone approached the telephone.

'Getting the equipment in now.'

'Everything all right?'

'Yeah, we'll start setting it up right away . . . hang on a moment. From what Mrs H. here is saying, number twenty-four was empty for quite some time, but then some men moved in ten days ago. She was out shopping on the morning of the snatch, so she didn't see anything.'

'Well done. Keep the line open.' Sykes signalled to the link controller to take it over. He then turned to the chief superintendent, who had just arrived. 'Could you consolidate your plain-clothes cordon immediately, and move in the other two observation teams. Video to go first.'

'They're ready now.' The chief superintendent gave a quick laugh. 'We'll probably have householders ringing in about all the shady characters in the street.' His remark was evidently not appreciated.

'Thirty seconds to twelve forty-five hours, Commander Sykes,' the DSL operations officer warned.

'Right, gentlemen, we're on camera.' Sykes leant forward to activate the switch marked COBRA. 'They can now see everything in the Cabinet Office briefing room,' he reminded them, glancing up at the round opaque eye.

A few moments later the Home Secretary's face appeared on the left-hand screen. 'We can see you and the operations table clearly, Commander Sykes. How's it going?'

'No hitches so far, Secretary of State. Perhaps the Commissioner would like to fill you in on the details.' Sykes took off his earphones and pointed out the correct switch. Afterwards, he beckoned to the fair-haired SAS liaison officer wearing a tweed jacket. The young captain bent forward with his hands on his knees so that his head was level with Sykes's.

'Is your Pagoda team ready?'

'They're in their telephone van waiting at the western end of Lime Avenue.'

Sykes turned to look at the planning table again so as to refresh his memory. 'You can bring them in closer now to be ready just in case we have a premature flap. We'd better leave the far side of the street to the observation teams, so let's say just short of number eighteen.'

Sykes found the Commissioner trying to attract his attention. 'The Home Secretary thinks we should impose the media blackout immediately. What do you think?'

Sykes replaced his headset with a sigh, forgetting that it would be picked up in the Cabinet Office briefing room. 'Frankly, Secretary of State,' he said, addressing the video screen, 'I'm not sure it's necessary until the last moment. All police vehicles have been prohibited from using sirens, and only veiled speech is allowed on the radio. Any reporters or broadcasting personnel found in the area will be detained until it's over. To be perfectly honest I'm worried that imposing a blackout might well spark some unscrupulous young reporter into trying to jump the gun somehow. It'll only be necessary if SAS or police movements become noticeable. And I certainly hope that won't happen.' Another television screen flickered to life in front of him. 'Ah, Secretary of State, we now have a picture of the house. This is transmitted by the camera in our second observation vehicle parked across the road. Are you receiving it too?'

'Yes. Looks as if the curtains are drawn in front.'

'I'm not absolutely sure about that,' Sykes replied, peering at the screen. It was an Edwardian semi-detached house in dirty red-brick. An unkempt hedge in front obscured most of the ground floor. 'Just a moment.' Sykes switched to the observation team's link controller. 'Tell team two to zoom in on each window in turn. And tell team three to report anything obtained with the directional microphones.'

'Roger, but no joy yet on sound.'

Sykes switched back to his COBRA channel. 'You'll be seeing the windows one by one in a moment, sir.' Once again conscious of somebody standing expectantly beside him, Sykes glanced up to see the chief superintendent.

'Our boys and the D11 marksmen have now taken up position in the three houses in Maltravers Road from where the rear of number twenty-four can be observed. The occupants have been co-operative, and the officer in charge is confident that no attention was drawn. Cameras and directional mikes will be in position in another ten minutes. By the way, we haven't received details yet on the civilian evacuation programme.'

Sykes looked at him sharply. 'There won't be one unless

surprise is lost.' He swivelled his chair and picked up the earphones again.

'But when the SAS teams go in . . .'

'Listen,' Sykes cut him short. 'Our men will be in the houses either side, in the ones across the road as well as in those behind. It is up to those officers to make sure that every non-combatant is in a place of safety. This operation has to be planned with the assumption that the SAS teams don't miss. Have you anything else to say?'

'No, sir.'

'Very well. Please let me know the moment the furniture removal van is ready.'

Sykes glanced at the digital clock in front of him. According to his checklist there was nothing to do for the moment except wait for the helicopters to land. He felt irritated and claustrophobic with all the liaison people around. Their interruptions seemed like futile attempts to establish the necessity of their particular role. It was probably something with which they hoped to impress their friends, Sykes thought, imagining the cryptic hints at drinks parties that they handled the crisis virtually single-handed. St Crispin's day in Whitehall, he thought contemptuously. The only real exception to the breed in Sykes's view was the quiet young SAS officer. They never seemed to be concerned by the opinion of outsiders. Sykes respected that. They got things done because they didn't keep looking over a shoulder the whole time to check on approval ratings. He was angered by the way certain people called them 'the Animals'.

He gestured to the captain to bring up a chair to the master console. 'I'd just like to check that our idea of the procedure still tallies with the SAS version.' The man nodded, ran a hand through his hair, then pulled his chair in closer. 'Now first of all your colonel will go straight to the Cabinet Office, won't he?'

'That's right. His job's to talk the politicians through the operation and stop 'em from getting too twitchy. With any luck he might keep them off your back as well.'

Sykes gave one of his rare smiles at this reminder that the Army disliked amateur interference just as much as he did. 'Well, I should be almost redundant by that stage if all keeps going to plan. Have you heard if the scale model is completed yet?'

'Not quite. It's a pretty crude mock-up because of the time factor. They're taking it straight to the house where the rehearsal is being carried out. Also it seems that the Lime Avenue house is similar to one of the layouts the teams have been practising on at Pontrilas, so that's a bonus.'

'Good,' Sykes said. 'Now it will take about twelve minutes to get the teams from the practice house to Lime Avenue in the removals lorry. So, to go on working backwards, how long do your teams need for practising?'

The captain sighed reflectively. 'Can't say for sure, but they shouldn't need much more than half an hour. Providing of course they can start straight away.'

'The bomb scare's been announced, and the whole area round the practice house is being evacuated now. And as a further measure, in case anyone sees the practice, all telephone lines from the district will be put out of action until your teams go in on the real thing. The Home Secretary has decided to use the media blackout legislation. Some of our senior officers are already on their way to the radio and TV stations where they'll remain until it's over.'

'One thing has occurred to me,' the captain said after a pause. 'How about turning the fake bomb scare in the area of our practice house into a real diversion. By that I mean pretending we think we've found the PM there so the terrs become convinced we're barking up the wrong tree.'

'The possibility struck me too,' Sykes replied judiciously. 'But on balance I think there may be a risk of trying to be too clever. You never know. The terrorists might only catch part of the broadcast and start watching out more carefully.' A buzzer sounded and a light began to flash on the console. Sykes fumbled with his headset. 'Yes, what is it?'

'The listening team have voices,' the link controller informed him. 'They think they caught a snatch of foreign language.'

'Shall I alert Mr Rayner?' the operations officer asked.

Having waited in an agony of impatience, Rayner responded with alacrity to the call from the operations room. When he arrived Sykes was fully occupied, so the operations officer briefed him quickly. According to the sound engineer, the quality of reception was not good enough to be relayed back over the rear-link. Rayner swore in frustration. 'But the listening team have it taped directly, don't they?'

'Yes, obviously, but there's no way of getting it out for the moment.' The attention of the operations officer was distracted by movements at the master console. The Commissioner, who had crossed to speak to Sykes, was now turning towards the door.

'What's happening?' Rayner asked.

'The Commissioner must be leaving for the Zulu Control vehicle at the end of Lime Avenue.'

'Oh, I must have a word with him before he goes,' Rayner said setting off after him. The operations officer was left there looking surprised.

The Commissioner only half-listened as Rayner walked rapidly at his side down the corridor explaining about the tape. He agreed impatiently when asked if there was a spare seat in his escort car. He was thinking how the whole security network had become even more labyrinthine now there was the Department of Security Liaison. And despite the reams of Responsibility Specifications which had been issued, it was still not clear who covered what in such a complex operation. But he had to admit with resignation that overlaps and duplicated functions were inevitable. He knew for example that his own foreign liaison group at the Yard had not taken kindly to the new organization. On an impulse that this was the right moment to demonstrate inter-service co-operation, he invited Rayner to come in his car.

When they reached the entrance, the Commissioner pulled on the civilian raincoat that his assistant held ready. 'Tell the escort car no sirens south of the Thames.'

On the way the Commissioner exchanged few words with his assistant and Rayner. They listened intently to the different radio nets. Unused to such journeys, Rayner was awed by the driving. He had never imagined it possible to cross London so fast in the middle of the day. It seemed only a matter of minutes before they were across the river. Just before Southfields the escort car pulled in to the side of the road allowing their Rover to speed on alone.

The moment they arrived the assistant took the hand microphone to inform Sykes back in the operations room. Rayner climbed out of the car and hurried after the Commissioner. The entrance to Lime Avenue was blocked with plastic cones and a 'Road Closed' sign. No uniformed police were in sight, only a number of men starting to break up the tarmac with road drills. Zulu Control was installed in an unmarked lorry next to the contractors' vehicles. Rayner tripped over one of the cables which spilt out in a twisted mass. The inside was lit by fluorescent panels. At the far end behind the driver's cab there was a bank of radio sets; the sides were covered in laminated maps.

'How are things going?' the Commissioner asked, leaning forward to examine the dispositions marked on the large-scale plan of the street.

'Seems all right so far, sir. All phones are now cut off except numbers twenty-two and twenty-four.' The chief inspector pointed up with his pencil. 'And our men are in all the designated houses.'

'No problems with any of the locals?'

'Just excitement at having ringside seats. It's a bit of a problem keeping 'em away from the windows.'

The Commissioner glanced round restlessly. He saw David Rayner standing awkwardly just inside the door.

'Oh yes, this gentleman needs the tape from the listening team in number twenty-four. The transmission was no good or something. What's the situation there?'

'Shouldn't be any problem. One of them'll be slipping out anyway to guide the military in.' He glanced at the clock. 'In fact he might as well do it now. The SAS aren't taking as much time for practice as we'd allowed.' The chief inspector took the microphone.

Rayner smiled his thanks. He was still amazed at his own nerve, or rather impulsiveness. He had no right to be there. The cluster of television screens opposite him showed both views of the house where the Prime Minister was held, the Cabinet Office briefing room, and the Department's operation room. He looked more closely. Sykes was no longer at the control panel. Rayner realized with sudden apprehension that he must be on his way over. Interfering in police work was the cardinal sin. And strictly speaking, he had no rights to the tape. Oh what the hell, he thought, convincing himself that nobody would be too concerned with bureaucratic protocol at such a time.

When the sergeant from the listening team arrived in his Gas Board overalls, the Commissioner pointed to Rayner.

'There's a second tape as well, sir. Some of it's in English, but most is beyond me. Sounds like German. Not that they said much. Er, you are with Commander Sykes, aren't you?'

'Yes, I am.'

'I can vouch for him, sergeant,' the Commissioner interrupted.

'Oh, that's fine sir. It was just that I was given orders that the tapes were to be delivered to Commander Sykes.'

Rayner thanked him for his help before turning to the chief inspector to ask whether the directional microphones had picked anything up.

'Nothing usable. The curtains are drawn at the back of the house, and that's where they are.'

Rayner nodded understandingly. He was just about

to ask if there was a car available when the radio came to life reporting the progress of the SAS in their furniture lorry.

'Christ, they really are ahead of time.' The chief inspector was visibly disconcerted. 'Why the hell weren't we told when they left the practice house?' A spate of orders for the cordon followed. Some three hundred armed policemen were on their way using a variety of routes.

'Well,' the Commissioner remarked, 'now's the time to start praying they don't choose the next few minutes to stick their noses outside.'

Eventually Rayner had to leave the control vehicle so as to make room for all those entering and leaving. Hunching his shoulders he tried to shelter from the wind. There had not been time to even think of bringing a coat. He watched the pale-yellow leaves spin down diagonally from the lime trees. They had already formed drifts in the gutters and on the pavements against the low garden walls. He noticed that the hedges had lost some of the geometrical perfection achieved during summer weekends.

Glancing around at the Edwardian houses, he remembered the problem of keeping the inhabitants away from their windows. Lime Avenue would certainly be world famous for more than fifteen seconds in its life. Perhaps those with video recorders would tape everything about it on television. The media of course would be furious at having missed such live drama, but they could not complain about the new legislation. In this case, with surprise achieved, the provisions were no more than a reassuring guarantee to the operational controllers. Little of that flurry of legislation had been used. The issue of identity cards was so far advanced that its completion was justified on the grounds of avoiding waste. Probably the most comforting aspect, Rayner thought, was that John Simmonds's unpleasant suggestion had been utterly disproved. Nobody had abandoned the Prime Minister to his fate. It was eerie to think of him held at gunpoint less than two hundred yards away. And the terrorists knew nothing of this small camouflaged army closing in around them.

Rayner swivelled as a car drew up sharply just beyond the other vehicles. Glimpsing Sykes, he had a ridiculous urge to hide. Any bravado he had felt evaporated on seeing that determinedly official face. Sykes hurried towards him talking to a fair-haired young man in a tweed jacket. Rayner immediately recognized the Army in mufti. Sykes looked up in surprise, recognizing his colleague.

'What are you doing here?'

'Well, at the moment I'm trying to get a car back to the – '

'Nobody will be allowed through until after the SAS has gone in. You'll have to stay here.' He did not need to add that undesignated personnel should never have entered the operational zone in the first place. Someone called out to Sykes from the back of the lorry. He acknowledged with a movement of his hand. He took another searching look at Rayner, then turned away.

Once Sykes had disappeared inside, Rayner calmed in resignation to the row that would ensue. He noticed the men around the entrance to Lime Avenue start to move. The sound of a large vehicle approaching could be heard. Rayner stepped out into the road so as to see better. A tall ungainly removals lorry came to a halt just before the corner. The policeman in Gas Board overalls ran across. One of the rear doors was opened for him from within. Rayner heard the thump inside signalling the driver to continue.

A few moments after the removals lorry had turned into Lime Avenue, police vans started to arrive. A uniformed sergeant approached Rayner, who brought out his identity card.

'You'll have to stay inside the Zulu Control vehicle, sir. No civilians of any category are allowed on the street.' Rayner warned him that there was not enough room inside. His heart sank once more as the man went in to check. He was directed back into the corner he had occupied previously. To his relief, Sykes did not deign to turn round.

Wedged in his corner, Rayner could just see the bank of television screens angled down towards those sitting at the narrow table. One of them now showed a bird's-eye view of roofs and streets. The police helicopter with its camera mounted was moving in closer. All the time the chief inspector seated next to Sykes recited events over the rear-link to the Cabinet Office. 'Explosive charges ready to blast connecting wall between houses. Audio equipment confirms space on other side unoccupied.' Rayner heard someone mutter that with the blast, the SAS would probably not need the flash-bang stun grenades. The chief inspector's commentary and the televisions reminded Rayner of the landing on the moon. It's not a bad comparison, he thought. There's little mission control can do now. He had to make an effort to visualize black figures in jumpsuits, balaclavas and gas masks crouched in flower beds behind garden fences. Rayner had not yet spotted anything on the screen showing the rear of the house, but a sudden movement on the one of the front caught his eye. The camera hidden in the vehicle across the street immediately zoomed in on the gate. Dark figures could be seen kneeling either side. One jerked his head towards the door. The two holding shotguns slipped forward to the limited shelter of the porch. The team leader checked his watch. On the SAS net he could be heard giving a countdown in a low voice. The two men by the front door raised the muzzles of their Remington shotguns ready to blast the hinges. The pair at the gate holding their Heckler & Koch machine pistols in front of them rose off their haunches like sprinters.

The microphones picked up the muffled boom of the charge a full second after the men with shotguns fired. They pushed in the front door and disappeared from sight. Rayner switched his gaze to the rear view of the house in time to see another pair of figures smash through the glass doors. Even the chief inspector's commentary came to a halt as he stared at the screens in the same agony of suspense as those around him. It was all so fast, and yet still seemed to take too long.

Then they heard the team leader's voice. He was trying to control his breathing. 'Objective secured. Hostage unharmed. Five out of five enemy negotiated. No casualties own forces.' Everyone in Zulu Control gave a spontaneous cheer of delighted relief. A hubbub of excited talk and handshaking followed. The Home Secretary appeared on the link from the Cabinet Office to congratulate all concerned. The Commissioner moved crabwise over to compliment Sykes, who did not turn away from the microphone.

'You are certain that there are no others hiding in the house.'

'I confirm, house clear. Out!' the SAS officer snapped back.

Sykes was unruffled. He called up the ambulance waiting to take the Prime Minister to hospital for a check up, then alerted a specially designated squad to remove the corpses.

The sudden deaths off-camera were forced on Rayner's imagination. Five unknown men shot down in a matter of seconds. He wondered how many of them had tried to surrender. Not that it would have done them any good. The risk of concealed weapons or explosives was the public justification, but however valid this might be, the automatic action was simply an unofficial death penalty. He had often heard the reasoning: 'Why waste a fortune on a trial. And then run the risk of a repeat performance aimed at releasing them once they're sentenced.'

'Come on, Dennis,' the Commissioner said, putting a hand on his shoulder. 'The chief inspector can take over now. You've done a magnificent job. Let's wander over and have a word with the SAS before they disappear for debriefing.' The Commissioner was then surprised to notice Rayner still there, but he assumed that Sykes must have asked him to stay. They were fellow group heads in the same organization. 'Wouldn't your colleague like to come with us?'

It was the first time Rayner had seen Sykes taken aback, and despite the situation, he could not help seeing its comical side. The customary lack of expression was quickly re-established on Sykes's face as he muttered something which sounded like agreement. The Commissioner's euphoria made him oblivious to nuances of atmosphere.

Rayner guessed that Sykes must be even more furious. He wondered if he had a vengeful character, but decided that it was unlikely. Such a man must feel that petty emotions were a luxury which interfered with the achievement of more important objectives.

Once outside, the three of them made their way towards the screens erected around the front of number twenty-four. The black-clad figures had removed the balaclavas and gas masks. Their faces shining with sweat, they looked incuriously at the new arrivals. Maclaren came forward expectantly. Rayner was struck by how young he looked. He found it unsettling in a strange way.

'Did you really suffer no casualties at all?' the Commissioner asked, surveying the close-quarter teams.

'Only some minor cuts from glass,' Maclaren replied with a nod towards one man with a field dressing strapped round a hand. 'Nothing else.'

'Well, you did a magnificent job, as I'm sure the Prime Minister has already told you.'

'He did seem pleased to see us.' The flat reply was evidently aimed to exclude the newcomers. 'Would you mind if we just got the weapons sorted out?'

'No, of course not,' the Commissioner answered. 'Please carry on.'

'Sarn't-major,' Maclaren called. 'Can we have the weapons checked and a provisional ammunition return.'

'Sir! Right you lot, get your used magazines cleared. Unused to the QMSI.'

'No for-inspection-port-arms?' one of the troopers asked ironically.

'Just get on with it, Jeffries. We all want to be away from here as fast as we can. Right now, ammo stakes.' The squadron sergeant-major brought his clipboard up into the ready position.

'Carlisle?'

'Fired four 5.56.'

'Jeffries?'

'Fired six.'

'Wilkins?'

'Fired eleven.' This reply was greeted with jeers.

'Oh dear, oh dear, Wilkins. Your round-to-kill ratio was a lot better on the last practice.'

'Yeah, but this was a fucking NO DUFF situation and I wasn't taking chances.'

'Chance shouldn't come into it. Not with a first-round kill, as I'm sure the QMSI has told you more times than he'd care to remember.'

'Anyway,' one of the others chimed in, 'none of the terrs got a shot off.'

'So bloody what?' Wilkins snapped back. 'We took 'em out before they had a chance. Well, didn't we?'

'Not that fifth one we weren't expecting. The dark-haired bloke hiding in that cupboard just like in the "ghost-train". He took an aim on me but his gat jammed. Christ, I nearly shat myself.' The close-quarter teams laughed loudly. Rayner watched Maclaren join in.

'What about me?' the man with the bandaged hand demanded. 'Could hardly hold the pistol grip, the blood made it so slippery. Thought I was going to have to chuck it away and give 'em a bit of thalidomide instead.' In the ensuing laughter it took Rayner a moment to work out the slang for unarmed combat.

'But the terrs must've been the ones shitting themselves,' Jeffries commented. 'They couldn't believe it when we came through that door.'

'Yeah, the first one I took out gave me such a goofy look I thought we'd hit the wrong address.' They all shook with laughter again. Excitement still lingered in the aftermath of tension. The downer would come the next day. Rayner tried to imagine the training which kept them at such a state for a momentary climax. In his National Service days the sergeants had yelled 'Mind over matter' at the recruits during endurance tests. But this group was different. They had been taught to detach mind from body in a way which had suggestions of eastern mysticism.

The observation helicopter continued to hover high above them. The thudding of its rotor blades became tiringly monotonous. Eventually an SAS trooper swore in exasperation. 'Hasn't anybody told 'em it's all over and they can piss off home.'

A plain-clothes detective appeared at Sykes's elbow. Rayner did not catch what he said because of another round of sarcastic cheers. Watching sideways he saw Sykes enter the house. Rayner knew he could not take this chance to slip away. He must wait to hear what had been discovered about the terrorists' identities.

A few minutes later the same detective appeared once more. Making his way straight to Rayner, he asked him to follow. At the entrance their feet crunched on broken glass. The front door which had been blasted off its hinges was leant up against the wall just inside. Rayner tried to see everything possible as he followed his guide. There were no carpets and furniture except for a solitary wooden chair in the front room. The old floorboards looked as if their colour came from ingrained dust and the cream walls seemed to have yellowed from nicotine. The bare rooms and the impassive faces of the plain-clothes policemen taking notes added a surrealist touch.

The detective led the way up the stairs, with echoing footfalls. It made Rayner think of the sound of empty changing rooms. On the landing, they stepped over the rubble from the party wall which had been blown in. Rayner peered through the hole to find a trim-bearded young constable staring back at him from the other side. In the rear room, Sykes was bent forward examining two bullet holes in the wall at stomach height. Beyond him a pair of detectives were cataloguing the contents of the room. The sleeping bags and tins of food made it look like the aftermath of a student occupation. Copies of the last few days' newspapers lay around untidily and cigarettes had been crushed out on the floorboards leaving small charcoal marks. Rayner was tempted to pick one up to see if it was a foreign brand.

Sykes looked round and straightened up. 'Ah, David. I hope your visit to the battlefield has been interesting.' Rayner smiled back warily. He would definitely have preferred Sykes's complaints out in the open, but the presence of subordinates made that difficult.

'Excuse me, sir.' One of the plain-clothes officers had appeared in the doorway. 'I've got all the terrorists' weapons and ammunition collected. Do you want it sent over to forensic?'

'We're not intending to put corpses on trial,' Sykes retorted. Rayner noticed the other detectives suppress grins like boys in class when one of their number is reprimanded. 'Just have them laid out along with all the other equipment, ready for the photographers. Then hold them at my disposal. We may need to send them abroad for examination and tests.'

Sykes nodded a dismissal before turning back to Rayner. 'I was about to say that we have something for you to get started on.' He handed him a paper with three names and West German passport numbers. Rayner looked up at him with a grim smile, but Sykes did not react. 'They're bound to be false,' he went on, 'but you can at least get preliminary signals off. Photos should be available for you later in the afternoon. We don't want to waste any time.' Then without waiting for Rayner to reply, Sykes told one of the detectives to organize a car for him.

More footsteps could be heard on the stairs. Sykes

controlled a look of exasperation on hearing the Commissioner's voice as well.

'Ah, there you are, Dennis.' The Commissioner acknowledged Rayner, who quickly explained that he was about to leave.

'We'll see each other back at the office then,' Sykes said. Rayner nodded in agreement before turning to follow the detective downstairs.

'So, he's off to go over those tapes from the listening team, is he?' The Commissioner's eyes were already darting round the room, so he did not notice Sykes's surprise. 'I'll have to be going myself in a few minutes,' he added peering down at the bullet holes. 'The Home Secretary wants to hold the press conference at half-past four.'

24

As soon as Rayner arrived back in his office, he asked Pannet to have copies made of the tapes. Once the originals were passed back to the police, he felt he could relax a bit more about the consequences of his impatience. Suddenly aware that he had not eaten, he asked his secretary to fetch some sandwiches. It was much later than he thought. He quickly rang the Intelligence Liaison Group on the internal telephone to give them the three sets of passport details. With the namecheck process under way he needed only to send a signal to Willi in Cologne. Having thus fulfilled his official role, he could concentrate on the tapes.

As he leant forward over his pad he imagined how that soulless building on the Innere Kanalstrasse would seethe at this apparent confirmation of German involvement. And with the computer system still out of operation, an air of suppressed hysteria was almost certain. Rayner felt guilty at the pleasure this image provoked; and these thoughts were not helping him write the signal.

A moment after Rayner had shaken himself from his fixed gaze at the opposite wall, his assistant strode into the room. He dumped the tapes on the corner of the desk. 'It's truly amazing. Anyone'd think a public holiday had been decreed in celebration. There wasn't a single bloody person around.' Rayner started to ask how he had managed to have the copies made, but his assistant did not wait for him to finish the question. 'Did it myself. It's not that complicated, and anyway, audio equipment's always been one of my hobbies.' Knowing his own uselessness with machines, Rayner was momentarily impressed.

Impatient to have Pannet out of the way, Rayner told him to go down to INTELLIG and keep the pressure on them. His assistant dashed off, enthusiastic that the group was at last involved actively. Rayner smiled faintly to himself, remembering the off-hand manner he had cultivated previously. He immediately put the duplicate tapes in his pocket, then returned to finishing the signal.

His external telephone rang. Still mesmerized by the words on his pad, Rayner reached automatically to pick up the receiver. He was confused to hear the voice of his counterpart in the *Verfassungsschutz*.

'David, I hope that with the real good news, you will not be still angry with me.' It took Rayner a moment to collect his thoughts and remind himself that it was now correct to play up the German connection.

'No, I never was angry with you, Willi. But as you can imagine it was a bit of a jolt to be told there was a total freeze on information at such a time.'

'I can imagine, but now things are okay, no?'

'Well, yes and no. I am in fact in the middle of drafting you a signal. Three of the terrorists had German passports.' Rayner paused to let the shock sink in. 'I know you can't help much, with the damage in the PIOS system, and that it's going to take you time to reprogramme. But unless we get full priority on assistance, internal inquiry or not, then I'll have to redirect the request via ministerial level.'

'All right, David. You don't have to turn my arm. You will have everything we can provide.'

Rayner enjoyed his role with a sneaking satisfaction. 'Listen, I'm sorry about putting things aggressively. But we've got to clear it up fast for the sake of Anglo-German relations.'

As Rayner replaced the receiver, the door of his office opened. Sykes entered still wearing his raincoat. Coming straight to the point he said that a major row had blown up over the tapes. 'I had not realized', he went on, 'that that was your reason for going, since you were not frank with me about it.' Rayner was about to say that there had been no opportunity, but deciding it was safer to keep quiet, let Sykes continue. 'Perhaps I should have worked it out,' the policeman said, sounding like an aggrieved schoolmaster claiming that a boy had betrayed the whole school. 'But I had more than enough on my hands at the time. Anyway, the Yard is extremely upset by what it sees as an unjustified interference.'

'Listen, Dennis. I'm very sorry if my misunderstanding has complicated matters for anybody. But the operation is over now, and we've got to get things cleared up quickly, as you yourself said.'

'Quite,' Sykes replied observing him closely. 'And time would be saved if agreed procedures were respected. You would have received copies, along with everyone else who might need them. All I can say is that I hope this self-awarded priority has proved worthwhile.' Even though he had not formulated a direct question, Sykes stared down at him waiting for an answer.

'To be perfectly honest,' Rayner said, affecting a deeply embarrassed manner, 'I haven't yet had a chance to listen to them because I needed to get those preliminary details you gave me off to Germany.'

'In that case,' Sykes retorted, 'I'm sure you'll agree that no more time should be wasted.' He reached forward to pick up the originals from the corner of the desk. 'The correct department at the Yard is waiting to analyse them. I'm sure that their interpreters are quite capable of doing the job.'

After Sykes had left, Rayner felt a fierce satisfaction. All right, you fat slug, he said to himself. Just let's see who comes up with the *correct* analysis. He strode through to ALLIG's general office to fetch the group tape recorder. On returning he locked his door.

But to his frustration, the quality was as bad as the sound engineer had warned. It was only possible to pick up snatches of conversation, and almost impossible to distinguish accents. At one point there were outbreaks of what sounded like tense laughter. Someone had said that they had better start rolling up their sleeves. Then another voice said ominously that the pig's blood had better be fresh. No other remarks seemed unusual. Rayner swore in disappointment when the tape came to an end.

Determined not to be thwarted, he thought of another possible source of information. After Sykes had entered the house at Lime Avenue, Rayner discovered the name of the young SAS officer, and found that before transfer to the close-quarter teams he had been in G Squadron, which consisted of Guards Division personnel. Rayner looked at his watch. It was tea-time. He reached for the telephone to ring Chelsea barracks.

'Officers' mess lance-sergeant Hawkins speaking *sir!*' a voice answered. Rayner smiled to himself. The Army had still not discovered punctuation except for the word sir. It brought back memories of having to yell name, rank and number in a breathless rush while balancing on the chicken run high above the assault course. 'Could I speak to Captain Wedderburn, please?'

'Who shall I say sir?'

'His cousin, Mr Rayner.'

'Sir!'

Rayner gave an amused sigh. He reflected on the automatic formulae, knowing full well the capacity of NCOs for polite contempt. It made him think of his cousin. Charlie was a bit of a pompous ass who made his friends laugh, but Rayner shuddered to imagine what the guardsmen said about him in their barrack room.

A rather flushed voice greeted him. 'What a surprise, David. How are you? And how's MI shush or whoever you're with? Still making sure we can all enjoy sweet intoxicated dreams in our beds at night?' He gave such a laugh that Rayner had to take the receiver away from his ear.

'Charlie, I wouldn't envy any red who tried to hide under your bed. Anyway, I thought you were supposed to be defending us.' Not wanting to bring out his request abruptly, Rayner was happy to continue the banter.

'Defending you lot? Hardly on public duties, lad. Our swords aren't exactly armour-piercing, you know. Still, makes you think. Bloody MoD will probably soon have us practising the Guard in nuke suits or whatever.' He gave another explosive laugh. 'Or maybe gas masks and bearskins. Make us look like Darth Vader in *Star Wars*. Give the tourist trade another boost. By the way, did I ever tell you? The Black Watch once had a gas mask specially designed so they could still be piped into battle even under NBC conditions. You should have heard what the bloody Yanks had to say about it on a joint exercise. They *simply* couldn't believe it!'

Rayner laughed politely. The risk of asking such a character as Wedderburn seemed foolhardy, but it was too late now. 'Charlie, I was actually ringing you to ask a favour.'

'Ask away, old man. What can I do for you?'

'First of all, you really must keep this to yourself. Seriously.'

'Silent as the grave and all that, I promise.'

'Do you know Jamie Maclaren in the SAS?'

'Of course, *mon cher cousin*. Went into the Coldstream. Second battalion. We did the drill course at Pirbright together. What do you want with the killer kid? . . . Oops! Suppose I'd better not ask. Must be very hush-hush. They're just down the road at the moment in the Duke of York's. Then I presume from tonight they'll all be taking a spot of leave. Hadn't occurred to me that you were involved in today's great deeds.'

'Charlie, *please*.' Rayner entreated. 'Keep this one quiet.'

'All right, all right. I may be a bit of a gasbag, but if I'm warned I don't usually drop bricks. Anyway, what do you want me to do?'

'I need to have an informal chat with him. Off the record and all that. Don't want to stir up inter-departmental suspicions. There's such jealousy . . .'

'Must be a positive snake-pit, old man. I'm sure I wouldn't last half an hour.'

'Best of all would be for us to meet on neutral ground. It would only take a short while. Do you think you could fix it?'

'How about a drink at my flat then?'

'Charlie, you're an excellent man. But ASAP, please!'

'Rightie ho. I'll call you back once I've got in touch with him. You'd better give me your number as I'm sure directory inquiries will deny all knowledge of you, double-o-seven.'

After replacing the receiver Rayner shook his head in wonder. He remembered Susie observing that Charlie had unashamedly nailed his colours to a stereotype. That was true of course, Rayner thought, but most of the time the fool was just taking himself off. Anyway, God help us when the Russians come.

25

While he took off his coat standing in the hall, David Rayner looked through the double doorway into the sitting-room. Susie was again wedged in the armchair head down over a book, with only the light from the table-lamp to read by. She just shook her head when he asked if she wanted the evening paper. Evidently she would avoid comment on the day's events.

Although such an insignificant gesture did not necessarily indicate hostility, he sensed it in the atmosphere. Instead of hanging up his coat, he laid it over the gift-wrapped flask of perfume from Harrods which he had left on the chair just inside the front door. There would be a more opportune moment later, he told himself. Or else he could just leave it on her pillow.

The telephone began to ring. Marking her place with a finger, Susie closed the book before reaching across in front of the lamp. She gave their number in a flat tone. Her impassive expression was disturbed by a twitch of irritation when she recognized the voice. 'Fine, thanks,' she said. 'David's right here.' She held the receiver up in the air without looking at her husband. 'It's your cousin Charlie,' she announced with a measured lack of enthusiasm.

David was taken off-guard, having wanted to consider things carefully before he proceeded. He hesitated, unable to decide whether to take the call upstairs. Then he advanced brusquely round the sofa.

'Charlie, hello. How are you?'

'All right thanks,' Wedderburn replied. 'Just rang to check that tomorrow evening around seven at my place is okay.'

'Sounds excellent. Much appreciated.'

'Marvellous. Look forward to seeing you then.'

Susie stared intently at her page as David replaced the receiver, greatly relieved by Charlie's unexpected discretion. He felt a strong need for a whisky despite knowing it would make his headache worse.

'That must be the shortest conversation he's had in his life,' Susie remarked without lifting her head. David looked at her in surprise for an instant, then gave an amused grunt. 'Yes, quite probably. Er, do you want a drink?'

'No thanks.'

As he turned away to fetch one for himself her eyes followed him. She exhaled slowly, despairing of his nerve. After the night before it had required willpower to throw him another line. But again he had walked away from it immediately. What the hell was she expected to do? If she had greeted him with a hug, he would either have stiffened in suspicion, or else felt stronger at her weakness.

'By the way,' she said, again staring at her page, 'I'm having dinner with Nancy on Friday night.'

'Oh?' He rattled the ice-cubes in his glass, forgetting as usual that it irritated her.

For a moment Susie was tempted to prolong the pause or pretend to be flustered. Serve him right, she thought, if he started to believe I was having another affair. But she knew such provocations belonged to the past. The trench-warfare days.

'John's got a do at his old college, so we're having a girls' dinner. Nancy insists I stay the night to save flogging all the way back afterwards.'

'Good idea,' he said, unable to muster any feeling in his voice. 'Should be a nice change for you,' he added making a further effort, but to little avail. He looked over at her evasively, then muttered that he had some work to finish.

After he had disappeared into the study, Susie slowly eased her rigidity in the chair. She stretched her legs, and felt the blood circulate again. Peering at the carriage clock, she saw it was almost time for the news. Despite her cynical comments she felt an urge to see the climax. It was a compulsion she rationalized unconvincingly as a fascination with drama becoming fact. She turned on the television slightly disappointed with herself, as she had been after listening to radio newscasts earlier. The excitement in the reporters' voices she found exasperating, especially since they had not arrived until it was all over. Almost as soon as the signature tune faded, the door of the study opened. David came in quietly and stood behind the sofa, without glancing in her direction. After refusing the evening paper, Susie felt as if she had been caught eating chocolates having said she was not hungry. They watched in silence as excerpts were shown from the video tapes recorded in the Zulu Control vehicle. Susie looked up over her shoulder and noticed David's tenseness. Turning back to the screen she caught a brief shot of the Prime Minister's arrival at the hospital.

'He doesn't look too great,' she commented quietly. There was a noticeable pause.

'Nor would any of us after that.'

26

Charlie Wedderburn had recently bought a first-floor flat just off Redcliffe Square. 'Convenient for the office, as they say,' he remarked. His cousin glanced round unsurprised by the two portraits of Victorian forebears, sporting prints and pastel-green walls. Rayner recognized the chintz on the sofas and chairs as almost identical to that in Charlie's family home.

'Bloody MO suggested that I should jog to work,' Wedderburn added. 'Obviously thought he was being funny. I suppose he expects me to go out and buy running shorts in Brigade colours like a squaddie.' He bent to switch on another lamp. Rayner laughed, imagining the sight, but then guessed his portly cousin looked odd enough already on London streets. His regulation civvies of bowler and pin-stripe suit nowadays probably attracted more stares than a punk. Rayner noticed how the red coarse flesh of Charlie's neck bulged over the starched collar. Voyeur's chastity belt, the guards officer had once joked.

'How's Susie?' Wedderburn asked with polite indifference.

'Fine thanks,' Rayner replied, remembering that it had also been her answer the night before. Wedderburn nodded perfunctorily as if accepting a corporal's routine report. He then examined his watch in the decisive manner of officers who know they are under observation. 'Jamie should be on time. When he does get here, I'll slide away. I'm sure you don't want me playing gooseberry.'

After a pause, Wedderburn gestured towards the newspapers on a sofa table. 'Not that Jamie's lot will get swollen heads, but the press has really gone to town.

Even more so, I'd say, than after that Iranian embassy thing. I'll probably have half the company forming up with applications for the selection course. Anyway, there's no doubt that it was a damned fine operation.'

Rayner murmured appropriate agreement, but Wedderburn had turned to look out of the window. The curtains were not yet drawn although it had been dark outside for over two hours. He stood to one side as if influenced by an atmosphere of conspiracy. Then noticing that he had too much cuff showing, he reached inside his jacket to hitch up his shirtsleeves from the shoulder.

'Aha! I have him visual.' Wedderburn's exclamation seemed to release him from the seriousness he had so recently established. He beamed at an astonished Rayner. 'Just practising my US militarese. Been detailed to look after some Yank colonel. You know, David, they really *do* say such things. I've heard it myself on one of those giant schemes in Germany. Wonder if they say "I have you aural" when they can hear you. Most unfortunate misunderstandings there.'

'I never knew you were so anti-American, Charlie.'

'An-*ti*,' he corrected the emphasis on his way to the front door. 'No, I'm not, old man. But I do think it's time we set up a committee on unBritish activities, and started locking up pop-singers, hamburger sellers, walkie-talkie freaks, and roller-skaters with those headphones and vacuous expressions.'

Wedderburn opened the door to welcome his brother officer. 'Jamie lad, good to see you. Come on in and let me introduce you.' He made it sound as if his guests had been longing to meet each other for years.

Maclaren followed him into the room. He appeared smaller in his plain suit, which looked off-the-peg in contrast to Charlie's blatantly tailored pin-stripe. He was slim, almost slight, and his smooth-skinned features were slightly feminine in quality. Certainly not your hairy-arsed para. Rayner felt almost certain that Maclaren must despise Charlie as a social dodo. But what had made

Maclaren join a Guards regiment in the first place? Rayner then wondered if his own reactions were conditioned by having last seen him sweaty and camouflaged. That had automatically made him appear the type who felt at home in an ice-hole in the Arctic or a sangar on an Arabian *djebel*; not wearing a suit around Chelsea.

Maclaren eyed Rayner briefly and acknowledged Charlie's introduction. Rayner felt a slight chill which contrasted strongly with the irresponsible banter of a few minutes before. On a dramatic impulse, he sensed that Maclaren had brought in with him the dangerous world outside. He remembered the precautions he had taken in case he was still being followed, and the new awareness that his telephone must be tapped at home as well as at the office.

'So help yourselves to drinks over there,' Wedderburn said looking from one to the other. 'Fine, well then. I'll just do my sharp turn to the right and fall out.'

Once their host had shut the front door behind him at the second attempt, Rayner moved towards the tray of drinks asking Maclaren what he wanted. When he requested a tonic water on its own, Rayner made a face to himself. He tried to imagine the regime of training which never lapsed. The thought of it made him feel even more uneasy.

'Er, why don't we sit down?' he suggested, returning with the two glasses. He gently swirled the ice-cubes as he reconsidered his opening gambit.

'Well, first of all,' Rayner said, forcing an informal tone, 'you must be wondering what this is all about.' He realized immediately that it sounded like a line from an old war movie. 'Since we saw each other in Lime Avenue,' he hurried on, 'the security agencies have had their time cut out trying to identify the terrorists, as I'm sure you're well aware.' Rayner knew that he should pre-empt any questions at least until Maclaren had settled into the routine. 'Now, you've been debriefed in detail already. Pretty exhaustively too, I'll bet,' he added with a sympathetic smile which was not acknowledged. 'And so you're probably surprised at this rather unorthodox approach. Well, the truth of the matter is that there's a certain amount of amour-propre holding things up. Some people, who'd better remain nameless, seem a bit touchy about the report on your debrief.'

'But surely it included a transcript verbatim.'

'No, only excerpts, so it wasn't as helpful as it might have been. In fact it left one or two questions unanswered. And the Germans are particularly keen on having things cleared up, as I'm sure you can imagine. I presume Charlie told you that I'm head of the Allied Liaison Group . . .'

'Not quite,' Maclaren said drily. 'I think he must have got your department mixed up with something else.'

'Perhaps Charlie was being security-conscious,' Rayner said with a quick grin, hoping to develop this hint of relaxation. But Maclaren gave only a polite smile in return.

'Well, anyway, if my group is going to scotch rumours which might severely damage allied relations, then I need to get things clear in my own mind first. My main interest, which the report does not cover, concerns the reactions of the terrorists. The efficiency of your teams didn't leave much to interrogate afterwards.'

Maclaren's expression disdained the last remark. This at least helped reassure Rayner that the most alarming possibility – SAS collusion – could be ruled out. 'Oh, yes, before I forget. In today's papers there was a suggestion that your teams had been switched around at the last minute. Where on earth do you think they got that notion?'

'I heard from our colonel that it must have been passed to the press by some government source. But the suggestion's rubbish . . . not that it makes any difference one way or the other.'

Observing him carefully, Rayner was again certain that Maclaren spoke the truth. The noise of an emergency siren came from a couple of blocks away. Rayner tensed instinctively, but then told himself it was only an ambulance on its way to St Stephen's. He saw that Maclaren was watching him.

'Right, my first and obvious question is whether the terrorists said anything when you all burst in. Did they surrender or shout slogans of defiance?'

'No. I never heard anything, nor did any of my men, from what they said.'

'Were the terrorists so taken by surprise? I mean did none of them try to kill the Prime Minister?'

'They got the freeze, as we call it. But that's the whole point of our tactics. The explosive charges, the magnesium stun-grenades, they're all designed to achieve complete disorientation for at least four seconds. And that should be enough for us to enter and take up first firing stance. By that point, the theory goes, the terrs should be more concerned with fighting us – the immediate danger –than dealing with any hostage.' Maclaren gave a slight twist of his hand. 'But there are exceptions, like the real fanatic. And of course we face major problems if the hostages are moved at the last moment, or if we can't get almost immediate access to where they're held.' He glanced down at his shoes. 'But this time it wasn't even Barricade and Hostage. We had complete surprise, in which case you can count on doubling the disorientation effect of the flash-bangs. And the team that came through the connecting wall from the next-door house was in the room in about five seconds . . . perhaps even less than that.'

Rayner was about to add that the terrorists would not necessarily have had their weapons to hand, but he decided that such an observation might not be tactful. 'So it was a copy-book operation,' he said instead, but Maclaren did not appear pleased.

'It was hardly an exercise where the enemy had a DS Pink telling them what to do.'

'It was a Directing Staff Yellow in my day,' Rayner could not resist saying. Maclaren gave another faint smile. 'But what I meant by "copy-book",' Rayner continued hurriedly, 'was terrorists acting as you would have expected.'

Maclaren looked surprised, then mystified. 'I'm sorry, I don't get you. What do you think might have been different?'

Damn, Rayner thought. I've put him on his guard. 'Nothing in particular. Just want to be absolutely clear for when I'm in the hot seat facing our allies.' Rayner was cautiously pleased so far, but warned himself against overplaying the ALLIG card. 'Now then, their weapons,' he hurried on feeling it was safer to scramble the sequence of questions. 'Did you happen to have a look at them out of professional curiosity?'

'I did examine a couple of them.'

'The police report is not very instructive, presumably because they haven't had enough time yet. Anyway, the serial number on one of the machine pistols recovered apparently linked it to a terrorist source in Italy.'

'And so?'

'But surely no terrorist with any sense is going to have a traceable weapon.'

Maclaren shrugged. 'Perhaps they didn't care, or didn't think they would be found out.' He noticed Rayner's look of scepticism. 'But having proclaimed their identity and aims so proudly in their communiqués, why should they be so concerned to suppress all connection with other groups in Italy, or wherever? I thought they went a bundle on the international bit. Besides, a terr doesn't usually start off on an operation imagining that his gun's going to end up as an exhibit in police headquarters.'

Rayner inclined his head. 'Okay, well then tell me about the guns you looked at.'

'I examined two. One of the terrs had a misfire.'

'The one who came out from behind the door, wasn't it?' Rayner asked. Maclaren eyed him suspiciously, before recalling that the incident had been mentioned in his presence. 'Yes, that's right. I checked the working parts.'

'And what did you find?'

'Both weapons were in good order and well maintained.'

'SAS standard?'

'I'd have passed them in a weapons inspection,' he replied evenly. 'There was nothing wrong with the firing pin.'

'So it was a dud round?'

'Yes, the percussion cap was scored.'

'And the explosive charges?'

'The terrs seemed to have known what they were on about.'

'I presume your boys carried out the make-safe drill. Was it primed? Ready to blow?'

'Not immediately, but that was to be expected. They'd have only had it fully prepared if they'd thought the house was surrounded. As far as they were concerned it was still a Hidden Hostage situation.'

Rayner nodded earnestly, then uncrossed his legs to lean forward with his elbows on his thighs. He rubbed his hands back and forth, staring at the carpet. He had covered everything he had planned, but felt some more questions were necessary so as to cover his tracks a little.

Five minutes later he noticed Maclaren slide his wrist forward dragging the sleeve to expose his watchface. He asked him if he was in a hurry.

'I'd better go fairly soon,' he replied. Convention seemed to demand a few minutes of non-shop talk, so Rayner asked if he wanted any more tonic. He shook his head.

'You know, I don't think I've ever come across two people more unalike than you and Charlie.' Rayner gave a forced laugh as if the joke was against himself. Maclaren shrugged imperceptibly to indicate that there was little he could say to that. 'Do you find you miss regimental life in London, at all?' Rayner added quickly, feeling a direct question was needed.

'I was never very keen on the "Sarn't-major this man's tunic is absolutely filthy" bit.'

'Yes, I suppose public duties must get very monotonous,' Rayner said lamely as if it had never occurred to him before. Maclaren's reserve reminded him of the scene in Lime Avenue. The young officer who distanced himself from fellow figures of authority while identifying with his teams.

Maclaren examined his hands, waiting to go. Rayner felt disturbed by his youth, as much as by the idea of him as one of the best-trained killers in the country. What does someone like that do later on? The Vietnam long-patrol boys had returned home to sit at the window following cars and pedestrians in their rifle sights. Later, he understood that it was Maclaren's apparent normality which unsettled him the most.

After Maclaren had left, Rayner sat down feeling weak. He could not yet cope with the half-formed suspicions churning in his imagination. He sighed pointlessly to the empty room, then looked around. He decided to wash the glasses and leave his cousin a note of thanks.

27

During the night David Rayner was sick. Nervous tension also made him sweat and shift uncomfortably in bed. He finally relapsed into a heavy sleep soon after hearing the first train in the far distance. The dreams which followed started with Deakin coughing blood into his hands. Then David saw that it was really Maclaren, and that the blood had disappeared. At some stage a dwarf had appeared whom he knew to be de Castezac.

When the alarm sounded at seven, David felt unable either to go back to sleep or to move. He lay limp and exhausted, his eyelids opening a little then closing again. He regretted that he had not asked Susie for a couple of her purple bombers. There was absolutely no question of going in to work, he decided. The idea made him feel better until he remembered he had missed the Friday before as well. And it was vespers again, or 'group-head pow-wow' as Pannet called it in his ludicrous attempt to create Departmental jargon.

He must have dozed off because the next thing he knew was a knock at the door and light from the window over the stairs. His eyes jerked open guiltily.

'Haven't you overslept a bit?' Susie said silhouetted in the doorway. He told her he did not feel well but refused her offers of aspirins or tea. 'Okay, I'll leave you to sleep,' she replied. 'Give a yell if you change your mind.'

Closing his eyes again David tried to work out why her manner, which had been neither solicitous nor harsh, struck him as unusual. But the effort of concentration was beyond him. He was also distracted by a tap dripping in the bathroom. Anticipating the next drop he could not relax, and had no energy to get out of bed. It was worse than the ticking of an alarm clock.

Soon after nine o'clock he knew it was time to summon the courage to call the office. Rayner's famous long weekends, he thought. After struggling into a dressing-gown he sat on the side of the bed. Instinctively he passed his hand over the lower part of his face. The skin felt raw and the stubble brittle.

'Feel any better?' Susie called on hearing him descend the stairs laboriously. He muttered a non-committal reply. 'Do you want any breakfast?' she asked but the idea of food reminded him of his nausea. He asked for a cup of tea.

Standing indecisively in the hall, he looked through the sitting-room at the door of his study where the tapes awaited him. He tried to ridicule the feeling that their presence posed a danger in the house like that strange sensation caused by Maclaren's arrival in Charlie's flat. An artificial security breached. All that crap about an Englishman's castle, he thought. No better than hiding under the bedclothes when you think you've heard a burglar downstairs. He was certain that a car had followed him back from London the night before. There was no way of knowing for sure it was 'the home team', as Deakin put it. But first of all he had to ring in so as to obtain 'the Direktor-Generalissimo's personal dispensation', in the words of that idiot Pannet. He felt sick of all the role-playing phrases.

To his astonishment, the director-general sounded very sympathetic. But then Rayner noticed a slight change in tone. The director-general said that his colleagues had noticed how he had been under strain recently. And in fact he had even intended to suggest a fortnight's leave. Pannet would therefore assume responsibility for ALLIG's routine functions until he felt up to it again.

Rayner stared across the room as he replaced the receiver slowly. He was certain that Deakin had warned them. Perhaps he had taped the conversation from under the seat, while the shadow on the moped was a complete fiction aimed to keep him in the car. At least Deakin was accurate about one thing, Rayner thought bitterly. I really did need a Personal Security refresher. He shook his head in anger at himself. It was even taught in basic training. To bring your subject's guard down, scare him, then change the location rapidly to somewhere which seems safer.

Susie, who arrived with his tea, was about to inquire if the office objected, when she saw his expression. She asked instead what the trouble was.

'Nothing,' he snapped.

'But you look as if they've just given you the sack or something.'

'Nothing's the matter!' he almost shouted. She did not flinch. She just put the cup down on the table and walked out of the room.

By the time he realized he should apologize, her bedroom door had slammed upstairs. He uttered a futile curse, wondering what to do. Finally, he told himself that the best course was to deal with the tapes first, because he would only be able to talk calmly afterwards.

Taking the blow-heater, he shut himself in the study. His main priority was to establish de Castezac's motives as well as his detailed plans. What did he want his men to do with the Prime Minister? Force the government to release the Irish prisoners so as to create a reaction against its weakness? Or was it really an assassination under false colours which would also provoke a useful backlash? Certainly in de Castezac's eyes, the Prime Minister was a red.

The evening before, Maclaren's manner had convinced him that the surprise had been genuine, thus preventing the death of the hostage. If that was the case, then those fiddles in the Black Orchestra died for very little. *Pour la patrie* in their definition of national interest. But there was precious little *gloire* in the tomb of the unknown terrorist.

He gazed out of the window at the wisps of smoke rising from their neighbour's bonfire, which still smouldered from the day before. The hedge of pastel-green cypresses they had planted for privacy needed several years to achieve their purpose. Rayner went back to stand in front of the blow-heater but it only burnt his calves, so he directed it at the chair. He had always wanted a bum-warmer and a real log fire for the study.

Feeling no further advanced, he leant over the arm of the chair to insert the tape from Lime Avenue. This time he ignored everything to do with accents or identities so as to devote his attention to the comments. And yet only the remarks about rolling up sleeves and 'the pig's blood' struck him as odd. Rayner played back each phrase of this section until he was certain of its meaning. Eventually, he sat back in his armchair. He went very still. One interpretation of their remarks suddenly made him remember Morgan's description of the Borghese affair in Rome. 'Oh, Christ,' Rayner whispered to himself.

Dennis Sykes was bent over his desk arranging papers for the group-head meeting later in the day. There was a knock at his door. He looked up to see Nigel Pannet.

'The director-general said you wanted to have a word with me,' Pannet explained, uncertain how to address him. Although he was now acting group head, he felt it would be distinctly premature to call him Dennis. Sykes straightened up, buttoned his jacket and asked him to take a seat. He had not yet had direct dealings with Rayner's assistant.

Sykes observed him carefully in the light of what he had heard. Cocky and irreverent, but only when no risk was involved. He watched Pannet's glance flicker round the office. It rested a moment on the large wallmap of London with chinagraph markings from the previous week's operation. Without thinking, Pannet reached into the side pocket of his jacket, but then stopped in the act of bringing out his cigarettes. The SESLIG chief's hatred of smoke had become well known in the Department. Sykes noticed the gesture without reaction.

He settled himself with his forearms on the desk and his hands clasped as if about to say a litany. Pannet eyed the pudgy face and glasses.

'Obviously you understand that our discussion must be treated as completely confidential.' He paused for Pannet to nod. 'Your group head claims to be unwell and rang in this morning to ask for leave, as I think the director-general has already told you. Now, from what I have heard and observed myself, David Rayner appears to have been acting rather secretively these last ten days or so. I was therefore wondering whether he might have mentioned anything to you which sheds any light.'

Pannet sighed as if to emphasize that it was a delicate matter. 'He's what I think you'd call a very private person in most respects. For example, I don't think I've ever heard him speak about his home-life.'

'I see. But would you have said he's been unusually preoccupied lately?'

'Frankly, yes. He's obsessed about something which he's refused to discuss with me. And . . .' Pannet made a reluctant face. Sykes urged him to continue with an impatient movement of the head. 'Well, I'm afraid routine work has suffered badly as a result. It's been almost impossible to get a decision out of him, even on those relatively unimportant matters which still require his okay.'

'And when did you notice this start?'

'Oh, about the time he went to France. I suppose we were all a bit on edge. And then after the PM's rescue he arrived back in a rather excited state. Dashing off instructions in every direction as if we were the nerve-centre. Copying tapes, priority namechecks through INTELLIG . . .'

'Copying tapes? What tapes were these?'

'The ones he was given at Lime Avenue,' Pannet replied in surprise. 'I thought he gave you the originals that afternoon.'

'Oh yes. Yes, he did. And I passed them back to Scotland Yard. They were rather upset at the mix-up. But what happened to the copies? Do you still have them in the group?'

'Haven't seen them,' Pannet replied turning down his mouth as he hunched his shoulders.

'Well, see if you can lay your hands on them. My group never received theirs from Scotland Yard and the director-general wants to listen to them.'

'And if I can't find them?' Pannet asked with an innocence which did not deceive the police officer.

'Then I'll ring David Rayner at home.'

Sykes proceeded to question him about the trip to Paris and Cologne. After that he dealt with inter-group matters, which evidently appealed to Pannet on symbolic grounds. Just before they finished, the external telephone on the desk rang. Sykes answered it, then put his hand over the mouthpiece. 'Er, Nigel, this is likely to be a long call. I think we can resolve any outstanding points later.'

As soon as Pannet had closed the door behind him, Sykes removed his hand to tell the caller to go ahead. After listening for a few moments he frowned. 'You're absolutely certain that it was Maclaren? But who's this Captain Wedderburn?'

Immediately after that call Sykes asked his secretary to get the adjutant of the SAS on the line.

28

The distant slamming of a door penetrated Rayner's consciousness. But by the time he had decided that the solid sound could only have come from the front door, he heard the starter motor of Susie's Mini. He rejected a pointless urge to check from the window. Whatever her destination, he would not be in time to stop her.

Rayner felt as if his limbs were empty. His weakness seemed like the exhaustion which comes from struggling for a logical argument in a dream. The previous evening's reassurance that his worst suspicions were unfounded now seemed harshly ironical.

The SAS teams had not been party to the whole psy-ops game-plan. Instead they had been an unwitting instrument in the scenario. As had de Castezac's men. Poor miserable bastards, Rayner thought with little pity. Like Borghese's thugs in Rome, they had no idea they were being used. And so, expecting to be given anaesthetic injections and splashed with animal blood for realism, they had sat waiting for the SAS to charge in. Then, presumably they had been told, the 'bod squad' would substitute real corpses, so that they could be smuggled out of the country. No doubt they would have looked forward to the Swiss bank accounts which had been promised them. But this time there had been no sympathetic officer to warn them of their true fate. It was the old rule. The real McCoy is always more secure than play-acting.

Oh, yes, he thought with bitter respect. It was all very cleverly thought out. The dud ammo, because as professionals they would have noticed if the guns had been fixed. The hint to the press that the teams had been switched at the last moment on the SAS colonel's orders, so that de

Castezac could be persuaded that an outsider had fouled it up. Oh, perfidious Albion, you have surpassed yourself, he murmured. How clever and patriotic to blame it all on foreigners. But there was just one thing you overlooked. Your dummies didn't know the game-plan went all the way, so they joked with first-night nerves, not having expected the microphones.

Rayner tried to grasp the mentality behind the whole operation. Did the covert world simply attract the devious, or did its nature corrupt recruits? The role-playing, the delusions of self-importance, the wishful omniscience, the conviction of their vital mission. Did all these things come about because such achievements could never be measured or acknowledged openly? The unsung hero's substitute drug. He thought of Deakin and his secret trophies associating him with power. But like Maclaren, to what sort of future could he look forward? Old comrade reunions nurturing old fantasies. Or straight to the great war-game in the sky? Redland and Blueland – Devils and Angels – them and us.

Later on Rayner went to fetch the newspaper from the kitchen, but he soon threw it down furiously. The media's euphoria of national self-congratulation had not abated. Rayner started to wander aimlessly around the house. His mood even began to make him understand Susie's hatred of the place. This reminder prompted him into considering her departure. She did not usually go shopping then, and it was far too soon to leave for her supper with Nancy. He opened the door of her room with a presentiment of disaster. Everything was abnormally tidy. Even the bedspread was smoothed right up to the cane headboard. The flask of perfume lay in its packaging on the pillow. Beside it was a note. 'David. Whether your remark the other evening was "stupid" or not is hardly the point. The perpetual lack of trust it exposed was painfully clear. Our marriage cannot be subject to a Rayner Official Secrets Act. I know your day-time world operates on a "need to know basis". Well, your attitude implies that I don't need to know anything. No relationship can survive in such a way. So until you feel ready to talk and to trust me, I don't see any reason to remain. I will ring tomorrow from Nancy's. S.'

It was completely dark when Rayner woke up in bed. He lay on his back trying to work out where he was. His mouth tasted sour, then he felt nauseated by the smell of whisky. He could not remember how long he had spent drinking or when he had crawled to bed. It took time before he could summon the will-power to roll on to his side. He stared at the discreetly lit digital figures of the radio-alarm. It was after ten.

Remembering Susie's note, he twisted his body round, sliding his legs to the floor. When he stood up there was a pain at the top of his head as if he had hit the ceiling. He moved stiffly towards the bathroom, stumbling over his shoes on the way. The strip-light over the mirror flickered into a painful brightness before he lowered his head into the basin.

Once dressed, he kept wandering back and forth trying to concentrate on what he needed. Finding his car keys took the longest. Downstairs, he went into the sitting-room where he dialled the Simmonds's number. It was engaged. He tried again immediately, but then deciding he could not wait, he went out to the car. Shivering in the seat, he started the engine, then ran his hand across his jaw. He remembered that he still had not shaved, but there was no time to go back. The headlights illuminated the gravel and grass as he swung the wheel, blinking to focus his vision.

On the road into London he had to brake hard several times after his gaze became fixated by the tail-lights of the car in front, but the possibility of falling asleep at the wheel did not frighten him. He told himself that he must ring, but every time he passed a telephone box, he decided on the next one instead. Later, when crossing Clapham Common, he told himself it would be easiest to stop in the West End on his way through.

After Hyde Park Corner he did a U-turn at the first set of traffic lights in Park Lane. A Mercedes pulled out from the kerb beyond the corner of Curzon Street. Instinctively Rayner swerved over to take the place. A taxi-driver behind hooted angrily. In the confusion of the traffic Rayner failed to notice a Ford Cortina with two men pass, then pull in beyond.

Without bothering to lock the doors, he weaved through the late-night crowd on his way to the brightly-lit entrance of the Hilton hotel. The lobby was virtually deserted as he strode through to the telephone booths. A young man at the reception desk looked up at him incuriously as he passed. As Rayner started to dial the number, he glanced hurriedly at his watch. To his dismay it was already midnight. He paused, then replaced the receiver to give himself a chance to consider carefully. He told himself that if he woke Nancy, Susie would be furious and refuse to speak to him. Still undecided, he felt like sitting down for a moment. Stuffed into a shelf under the telephone was a copy of the evening newspaper, which he took with him on an impulse.

Rayner sat on the imitation-leather banquette ignoring the subdued groups who waited for the lifts after an evening at the theatre. Then he picked up the paper to glance at its front page as if something there might help him arrive at the right decision. The large headline declared: 'THE PM IS BACK!' A photograph showed him on the steps at Downing Street with one arm raised in a wave. The phrase also served to emphasize the dramatic change in the opinion polls. Rayner made a sceptical face thinking that it would be only a temporary phenomenon. But then he started to wonder how true that was. He could only be certain that the man's most pressing concern lay not with the electorate, but within his own Cabinet. Somehow Maclaren's comment on facing the more immediate threat passed through his mind.

Leaving the newspaper on the seat, he found himself wandering back towards the car. On the pavement near the bus stop he bumped against a man, who swore at him assuming that the glazed stare was due to drink. Rayner climbed into the car like an automaton. He stared blankly ahead through the windscreen. For the second time that day his limbs felt numb and drained of any strength.

The most immediate danger to the Prime Minister's position had come from colleagues who wanted to depose him before the next election. But now there was no way they could press for his removal. Above all, the guns of his most bitter rival had been firmly spiked.

To have outmanoeuvred his foe successfully would certainly give the Prime Minister great satisfaction, but Rayner was sure it went much further than that. The old warhorse had a patriarchal attitude towards his party. His years of service were a constant theme in his speeches at Conference. Almost certainly he had a dogged belief that to surrender the leadership to his enemies would expose the Party to perversion and perhaps eventual destruction.

So if the Prime Minister was prepared to defend himself at any cost, a pact with the hawk faction in the security services possessed a devious logic: the emergency legislation they wanted for dealing with the increased unrest, in exchange for his political survival.

The hardliners must have included Deakin, Rayner reflected, too shaken to be bitter. And Sykes of course. Now it all started to make sense. The Home Secretary was the only minister the PM could trust completely. And he was the ultimate controller of the Lime Avenue operation. *Sir Neil, would you have any objection to Commander Sykes running the show?* Jesus, Rayner murmured to himself. De Castezac and his men really had been tricked. So much for the coup against a 'red' Prime Minister.

Rayner felt mesmerized as the implications of the plot penetrated his consciousness. Politicians usually overrated their ability to control the tiger they had decided to ride. Not only had the hawks obtained their security measures; they had almost certainly acquired a whip hand over key government leaders for the rest of their careers. Deakin would probably call it 'an all-round win situation'. Not devils and angels. But Mephistopheles and Faust.

Rayner lost all sense of time as he sat there oblivious to his surroundings. When later he started to look about him, the sights struck him almost as they would an infant out for its first car ride. The pedestrian traffic attracted his attention first. Drunks from a company dinner puffing clumsily at cigars. A croupier with a fur-lined car-coat over his dinner jacket. Young couples walking together like Siamese twins. Rayner watched a girl grin up at her boyfriend, wrinkle her nose, then take out her chewing gum to pop it into his mouth. Normally Rayner would have gulped with instinctive distaste, but he observed everything as if his windscreen was a television. Ahead, over the cars parked in front, he gazed at another hotel with pink-gold floodlights and national flags illuminated from below.

A rap on the passenger window made him turn his head. He saw a girl's face looking in at him with a questioning smile. He stared back at her. She opened the car door, then slid into the seat beside him.

'Looking for company?' she asked scarcely regarding him.

'Company?' Rayner repeated the euphemism with distant consideration.

'I can offer special services,' she added glancing out through the windscreen. Then she checked over her shoulder as she recited them rapidly like someone selling a household appliance, bored with listing its different functions.

'Are you watching out for the vice squad?' Rayner asked.

'Yeah, the mustard car,' she said disgruntled by his interruption. 'That's its colour.' She looked at his face, then seeing it registered no interest, her lips curled down in derision. 'I thought your sort liked being caned,' she said with a shrug before reaching for the door handle.

29

The next morning Susie awoke to a smell of roasted coffee from downstairs. To her surprise she had slept well without pills. The frustration that had kept her tense for many nights seemed to have been left behind in Woodside Close.

On her way down the twins brushed past her giggling. Nancy greeted her with an expression of mock suffering and demanded why her children's bio-rhythms had to be the exact opposite of her own. Susie offered to take them off somewhere for the morning, but Nancy told her to relax with the paper and have some peace herself.

'I'm not sure that a quiet life is the answer,' she said sitting down at the stripped-pine table. She remembered her remark to David the first time she came to the house. Nancy tilted her head to acknowledge that she might well be right, then carried on repacking the freezer in silence as she considered Susie's future.

'Yuk!' Susie exclaimed reading a short paragraph in between sips of coffee. 'What a way to go. There was a heroin smuggler who'd swallowed little bags of the stuff, and they burst inside him. Sounds like one of those moral tales brought up to date.' Nancy reacted with a suitable expression as she closed the top of the freezer. She then crossed to the oven to shake the trays with the coffee beans.

A few minutes later Susie interrupted her thoughts again. 'Hey! Guess what. You remember my awful joke that time David and I had supper here.'

'John was much worse as I recall.'

'Glad to hear that. Anyway, the PM's popularity rating has gone shooting up.'

Nancy moved the frozen container to the draining board then regarded her carefully. Susie looked back at her thoughtful expression with an air of amused inquiry. 'So what's the question? Where do I go from here?' With a movement of her head, Nancy acknowledged that that was more or less what she had been thinking. Susie stared down at the floor. 'Who knows? The ball's in David's court now.'

Late in the morning Susie rang Woodside Close, but the number was engaged. She was about to try again, but at that moment John arrived back from Oxford. The excuse for a postponement gave her a great feeling of relief.

It was one of those autumn Saturdays when dusk seemed to approach at lunchtime. John described his college dinner, embroidering it with several slanderous sketches. He then brought some white wine back to the sitting-room where they sat drinking. Nancy recounted his complaint that the bright greens and white made it look like the reception area of a design studio. Susie gave a polite laugh. 'I'd rather that any day than . . .' She stopped, then looked away from the two of them on the sofa. 'I don't think I can face going back.'

John suppressed a sigh of irritation. He had visions of Susie remaining on their hands for an indefinite period. After a short silence Nancy asked whether she wanted to try the number again.

'Yes, I'd better,' she said, pulling herself reluctantly to her feet. She crossed to the table by the door and dialled the number. Nancy was reminded of how they had sat in the same place when David telephoned home. She gave John a warning look which provoked a small grimace in reply.

'At least it's ringing this time,' Susie remarked with little optimism, but then concentrated expectantly when the receiver was picked up at the other end. The note of surprise in her voice checking that she had the right number made them both look round.

'Police? But . . . what's happened?' she demanded in alarm. 'I'm Mrs Rayner, so will you tell me what's happened!'

From the sofa they could hear a man's voice without distinguishing any of his words.

30

Sykes had to restrain his anger when one of the Special Branch officers came to the study to warn him about the telephone call. He stopped himself from demanding what a local constable had been doing by the telephone in the first place. 'Tell their chief inspector as diplomatically as you can that the house is our concern. They deal with the body, and nothing else.'

As soon as the plain-clothes sergeant had departed, Sykes played another section of the tape. It was undoubtedly the one recorded in Lime Avenue. He stopped the machine, then extracted the tape to put it in his pocket.

'Is that his wife?' Sykes asked, pointing to the framed photograph on top of the desk. Pannet looked up from where he squatted by the open drawers. 'Probably,' he shrugged. 'I never met her.'

Pannet continued spreading the papers on the floor as if searching for a joker in a pack of cards. 'Eureka!' he exclaimed suddenly without turning round. 'Here's a letter from his solicitor. Lamb as in baa-baa. Chancery Lane.'

'Good. Well, take the details,' Sykes replied. 'Then get on to them to make sure that he hasn't left anything with special instructions.'

The plain-clothes officer returned to inform Sykes that the nearest Saturday collection was from a post office seven miles away. Sykes told him to find something with Rayner's handwriting and to make a sample of the typeface from the portable Olivetti on the desk. Then he was to organize an examination of all mail in boxes within walking distance in case Rayner had slipped the observation team after his return from London in the early hours.

It was now established that he had definitely not left anything in the Hilton. And the plain-clothes officers had proved themselves more than thorough. They even arranged the arrest and search of the prostitute after she stepped out of Rayner's car. Sykes's gaze was again drawn to the dead man's personal effects, which lay sealed in plastic bags on the table. There were grounds for optimism, he told himself.

He noticed Pannet bend down to examine the old leather gun-case. 'Don't touch it, Nigel. We'd better have forensic confirm that there are only his fingerprints on it.' Pannet stepped back abruptly, then nodded in agreement.

'Who do you think F. Rayner was?' Pannet asked, indicating the scuffed black letters on the lid of the case. 'His father?'

'Probably his grandfather, judging by the age of the gun.' Sykes's tone indicated little interest in the subject. He was thinking how fortunate it was that the observation team had not followed Rayner closely into the wood, where they might have tried to prevent him taking his own life.

At first Sykes had been worried because no trace of a suicide note could be found. But then, having seen the body dressed for shooting, Sykes understood. Rayner's desire to camouflage his death as an accident only confirmed Sykes's disdain for the diplomat. The policeman turned his head to look through the sitting-room to the hall beyond, where the search team was being briefed. The house was nearly twice the size of his own, Sykes noticed. For the first time he felt a personal anger against Rayner's privileged scruples, particularly since the man had never managed to hide his instinctive distaste for the technicians of security work.

Susie leaned forward impatiently in the passenger-seat peering through the windscreen. 'We're almost there,' she told John. He acknowledged with a tight smile. The headlights refracted in the rain and the monotonous noise of the wipers had been a strain. 'God, you'd've almost thought it was night-time already,' he said.

When the end house of Woodside Close came in view they all stared apprehensively at the mass of vehicles. A motorcycle policeman with the rain running off his waterproof jacket waved them down at the roadside, but when John slowed, Susie ordered him to drive straight up to the front of the house. He braked to a halt on the gravel. Susie jumped out then, hunching under the rain, dashed across the headlight beams. Nancy shifted awkwardly across the back seat to follow her.

John looked round, wondering whether he would be allowed to leave the car there. So as to see more, he wound down his rain-spattered window. All the lights appeared to be on in the house. At one of the downstairs windows he recognized the face of one of the police officers who had interviewed him in hospital. John twisted his neck further on hearing purposeful footsteps on the gravel as the motorcycle policeman approached. They sounded like an accompaniment to the rain beating on the car's roof.

When Susie ran into the hall, she stared in horror at the men silently stripping the chairs and sofas. All the pictures had been removed from their frames and part of the carpet rolled back. For a wild moment it even occurred to her that David had called in a removals company. Nancy arrived behind her and also began to survey the scene. But she swivelled on hearing a radio crackle to life in the police car parked by the front door. Her attention was then caught by the zigzag ingots of mud just inside the entrance.

Suddenly Susie turned to run upstairs in the belief that they might have put him there. Breathing heavily, she wrenched open the door of his bedroom. The contents of the drawers had been emptied on to the floor and then rummaged through as if by a burglar. She crossed to her own room, finding it in a similar state.

On the far side of the bed a man was taking the drawers out of her dressing-table. He paused to look over his shoulder incuriously. By the bedside table stood a young man with dark hair and a brown moustache. His clothes were formally casual. A sports jacket, white shirt and navy tie with a motif. He held the flask of perfume which David had given her. The packaging lay in pieces on the bed.

'What the bloody hell do you think you're doing?' Susie shouted at him. 'Why are you treating him as if he was a traitor?' The officer regarded her with one eyebrow slightly raised. Then he turned to exchange glances with his colleague. Susie snatched the flask of perfume from his hands and left the room.

Not knowing where to go, she stopped on the landing by the window. With all the lights on in the house, it now looked completely dark outside. But putting her face almost to the glass, she saw the black cloud broken along the horizon with chinks of light. A moment of faintness came over her. Impelled downstairs by a frantic urge for fresh air, she rushed past Nancy to the open front door. The policeman on the steps moved to one side. Susie stood beside him and breathed deeply with her eyes closed. Eventually she opened them, staring out beyond the parked vehicles at the steady rain. The policeman eyed her uncertainly.

After a few moments Susie's breathing calmed. She swallowed before asking in a controlled voice where her husband had been found. The policeman leant slightly towards her to point out the white tapes marking a route across the field; it looked as if he was giving her street directions. Susie nodded then walked out into the rain apparently unaware of the glances from the police by the cars.

She climbed the fence into the field with slow deliberation, then followed the tapes which stretched forward at waist height into the darkness. The disorienting effect of the rain increased the sense of unreality. With her wet clothes and hair plastered to the contours of her head, she scarcely noticed slipping in the mud of the churned-up route. Below the silhouettes of the trees ahead she saw torch beams twist and flash. A little closer, she heard the clipped voices and mush of radio traffic, then she was able to distinguish uniformed policemen in black waterproofs and rubber boots. They had already begun to gather up the tapes around an area of trampled earth and disturbed leaves.

Susie flinched when a torch was shone in her face. The sergeant asked if she was Mrs Rayner. They had evidently been warned of her arrival by radio.

'Is this the place?' Susie asked.

'Yes.'

'Who found him?'

The sergeant hesitated before answering that he did not know. He seemed about to add something, but decided against it. Instead, he said: 'We're finished here now, Mrs Rayner. So we'll be making our way back to the road.'

'That's all right. I want to stay for a little on my own.'

'But you've got no light . . .'

'Please! Just leave me alone.'

After a long pause, the policeman assented uneasily, then gestured to his companions. They departed, rolling the white tape back on to large cardboard spools as they went. The sound from branches scratching against their waterproof jackets soon faded. Susie became aware of how tensed her body was. She discovered as the rigidity eased that her left hand still gripped the flask of perfume. With a clumsy effort she threw it into a tangled mass of bramble to the side.

Alone in the dark, she breathed in the smell of mud and wet leaves. It was typical of David, she thought. He wouldn't ever have done it in the house. Not with the possibility of someone close to him having to face the mess. Susie could not stop herself from thinking of Gerald's old boyfriend, who had put a cardboard grocery box over his head before pulling the trigger. She did not notice the warm tears which had started to roll down her cheeks.

David had even gone to great lengths to pretend it was an accident. That was a final attempt to ensure she didn't feel responsible in any way. It took Susie several seconds before she recognized Nancy's voice in the distance calling her name. She hesitated before turning back in the direction of the road.